SISTER SPIT

SISTER SPIT

Writing, Rants &
Reminiscence from the Road

Edited by Michelle Tea

San Francisco

Cover art © Cooper Lee Bombardier
Cover design by Linda Ronan

This book is also available as an e-edition: 978-0-87286-593-8

Library of Congress Cataloging-in-Publication Data
Sister spit : writing, rants & reminiscence from the road / edited by Michelle
Tea.
    p. cm.
 ISBN 978-0-87286-566-2
1. American literature—Women authors. 2. Feminist literature—United
States. 3. Lesbians' writings, American. I. Tea, Michelle.

 PS647.W6S56 2012
 810.8'09287—dc23

                                        2012019960

City Lights Books are published at the City Lights Bookstore,
261 Columbus Avenue, San Francisco, CA 94133.
www.citylights.com

Contents

Introduction

I'm writing from inside of the 2012 Sister Spit Van, careening down the 5, on our way to a show tonight at UC Santa Cruz. The students have requested that we all talk about class. Sister Spit has never taken a request before, but this is easy — most Sister Spit shows are about class. About class and being female, or about class and not being female, about being trans, a faggot. There is feminism in everything, a punkness too. What's funny is that everyone is sort of perplexed about what they should do to fulfill this class requirement. One person reads every night about her broke family and the weird ways they got by in 1990s Long Island; another reads about waiting on Castro clones at an all-night diner in San Francisco. What about the performance artist who goads our audience — so far, California college students — to put money into the carved-out crotch of a baby doll? Or the slam poet who lists the extreme ways his immigrant family reused every bit of plastic packaging they brought into the house? It's funny that there would be any stress about selecting a piece that explores class, but when it is wound so intimately into the fabric of your person — and hence, your art — it can be as hard to recognize as your own speaking voice.

But we all hear each other, here in the van. *Yeah, do that piece! Yeah — talking about having sex with a homeless person is totally about class. Yeah, that song you sing about working at the farmer's market counts as a piece about class.* And so we bring our show to a packed auditorium at UC Santa Cruz and without really trying become the embodiment of so much of the theory these kids are being taught. In the morning we convene with students and again discuss class. The things we share blow some of the students' minds, but our minds get blown, too. I have a major revelation, sitting there in this beautiful, wooden queer center, Redwood trees soaring outside the grand windows. *If I'd gone to college, none of us would be here right now.* Holy shit, it's true.

Back in the 1990s, Sister Spit is what I did *instead* of going to college. Almost twenty years later, I'm still doing it, now bringing our lived example of outsider experience, of different ways of existing, living an artists' life, directly into universities nationwide. Every year I cull a different group of writers and performers from the wide pool of underground geniuses I'm deeply fortunate to know. For one month we live together in a van. We take to the stage every night and bare our souls, expose our experiences in ways so unusual and artful it looks easy. We sell chapbooks, zines, books, and CDs from a table at the back of the room. We sell glass bottles for wishes, we sell posters and tote bags. Then we pack it all back up in our rolley bags and move onto the next town.

Sister Spit was born in 1994, to fill a void. Spoken word cresting in popularity in cities and college towns across the United States, with Lollapalooza recruiting performance poets to open up for the Beastie Boys in stadium shows and Poetry Slam about to demonstrate that literature can have the energy of a sporting event. In San Francisco there was no lack of poetry open mics for aspiring writers to show their stuff at, but the majority of writers hitting those stages were men. And not just men — dudes. Bros. Guys who set their beer cans at the altar of Charles Bukowski. Guys who ripped off their shirts and hollered their poems in homage to Henry Rollins. The events, be them in coffee shops or dive bars, had the vibes of a wild west saloon, and to get respect (or even get heard) you had to be bold enough to climb onto the stage and tell the ruffians sucking down suds to *Shut the fuck up.* They would startle quiet at your language, and then you had about twenty seconds to make them laugh or make them mad, to gross them out or piss them off. If you pulled this off you got a round of applause and/or some guy wanting to get in a shout fight with you at the end of the bar. Other poets would walk up to you and shake you hand, give you their chapbook; in another month you'd have one to give to them. The host would invite you to "feature" and you'd be paid in drink tickets. I loved this world, and the few females who figured out how to work the circuit were for sure the crazy bitches you wanted to be hanging out with — girls who'd gone to jail for stabbing their boyfriends, hookers, butch girls with cut-marks on their arms, junkie bike messengers, spastic fantastic jabber-mouths, brave, brave females and the best writers in the scene.

But what about the rest of the girls? In San Francisco, a city known for both its literary and queer scenes, why weren't there more females at these readings? Well, duh. Not everyone wants to have to tango with a bunch of drunkards to read their work. And work that's being honest about female experience in America can be hard and vulnerable; quiet and fragile. These bars were no place for work like that. Not to mention all the offensive poetry you had to endure waiting for your shot at the mic, poems where guys talked about women in ways were astoundingly retro and disgusting. I got in fights with male poets all the time at these open mics; I was into it. But not everyone has such a hobby. And so with Chicago poet Sini Anderson, Sister Spit was born. A girls-only open mic that ran every Sunday night, for free, for two solid years. By girls we meant past, present, and future females, and men were allowed to perform if they were part of a female's act. Once a year, on Easter Sunday, we'd have a marathon event called Sissy Spit, where all the guys we really liked would read.

The night of the very first Sister Spit, fifty females signed up to perform. We were unable to fit them all into the program. Our audience pushed back through the bar and spilled out onto Valencia Street. We had poets and writers and a puppeteer who crawled under the stage and performed a play with Nun finger-puppets. And off it went from there: a performance artist covered the stage in trash bags in anticipation of the mess she would make chain-sawing a pig's head, but then an animal rights activist *stole* the pig's head right off the stage and ran down the street with it. Girls danced naked with fire. A woman came every week and spoke to the Goddess through a telephone-shaped rock she'd found in the desert. Girls sang songs on acoustic guitars. Eileen Myles read with us, and Mary Gaitskill. Strippers took glitter baths in inflatable bathtubs, and drag kings masturbated dildos. A punk poet safety-pinned her lips shut, and we all dreamed of David Wojnarowicz. We had our canon — David, and Dorothy Allison, Jean Genet and Violette Le Duc, Mayakovsky and Cookie Mueller, Divine and Karen Finley, Diamanda Galas and Richard Hell, Emily Dickinson and Patti Smith, Kathy Acker and Sapphire, Kathleen Hannah and Aaron Cometbus, Ginsberg and yeah, Bukowski.

Oh excuse me — it is so hard to get any work done while *inside* the Sister Spit van! Dorothy Allison just stuffed her ear bud into my ear so I could listen to a bit of Joan Jett. How did we get from a weekly event that had us negotiating with venue owners about the fire hazards and underage girls Sister Spit shows brought into their space, to today, 2012, hopping between universities with Dorothy Allison lounging in the van beside me?

After two years of hosting our weekly event, Sini and I were burned out. We called Sister Spit quits and took a break. I started playing drums in punk bands. I wasn't great and neither were my bandmates, but that didn't stop us from hitting the road on a month-long tour up and down the West Coast. Riot Girl and Homocore were still raging — we played the Supergirl Conspiracy conferences in Santa Barbara and Seattle; we were part of a festival in Portland that Sleater-Kinney headlined; we played at the famous Capitol Theater in famous Olympia, Washington, and members of Team Dresch were in the audience. We made enough money to gas the van, and that was it. We slept on the floors of strangers. We drank their beer and bummed their cigarettes. I remember selling the book I was reading to a used book store so I could get five dollars. I remember scraping nickels together and purchasing a granola bar from a Plaid Pantry, my breakfast, lunch and dinner that day.

When I got back to San Francisco I was exhilarated, and bummed. Bummed because I had to quit my band — we were a dysfunctional family, and I couldn't take it. Also, after all the easy camaraderie I found with other poets and writers, the snootiness of the music scene was an annoyance. I put down my drumsticks and returned to my notebook. I met up with Sini and some friends at a Mexican restaurant to regale them with tales of my travels over margaritas, and the idea for Sister Spit's Ramblin Roadshow hit us in a burst of drunken genius. By my sorry standards, the punk tour I'd just survived had been a success! I'd seen parts of the country I'd never known. I'd spied what the larger queer scene looked like, I felt the thrill of performing for crowds of strangers. I woke up on the shag-carpeted rug of a punk house feeling worldly and wise, like a train hopper or a real beatnik. I felt freedom, and it felt *rad.*

If my crappy punk band could go on tour, why couldn't a bunch of poets? The writers I'd come to know through Sister Spit were *way* more talented than my band. And unlike the band, which relied on an audience who enjoyed our particular brand of obscure, noisy, atonal, instrumental math-punk, the stories and poetry of the writers we knew had a more universal appeal. Sini and I went to work booking a one-month national tour.

It is worth mentioning that I made $12,000 that year, and Sini no doubt made the same, if not less. We did not have cell phones (nobody did). We did not have credit cards. We did not have college educations that had empowered us to think we could take on such a crazy, ambitious project (and we also had no student loan debt shackling us to a straight life). We came from alcoholic families that had raised us to thrive in chaos and act without a lot of forethought. Thank god! If we had known we were setting out on what would be a $10,000 adventure, we would have *never* taken it on. But we didn't know anything. Town by town we booked shows, mapping our way across the USA. We turned to punk bible, *Book Your Own Fucking Life*, a how-to guide for touring bands published by Maximum Roc N Roll. We cracked open the cheesy *Damron Traveler*, the gay travel guide that always had a tanned fag by a swimming pool on the cover. We used it to hunt down gay bars across America, keeping an eye out especially for places that had drag shows, figuring they'd have a stage and PA. We sought out Slam Teams in cities and towns and asked them to book us a show. We began a steady fundraising cycle — one benefit a month for the first six months, upping it to two benefits a month as the tour grew closer. One benefit would be a spoken word show; the next a rock show. We had a big dance party that netted us a whopping $1,000 (the cost of our van!) and a fancier performance where Annie Sprinkle let us auction off a pair of her pasties. In August, we hit the road with a lineup that included Eileen Myles, my favorite writer *ever*; Ali Liebegott, my other favorite writer and also best friend; Harry Dodge, the performance artist who ran the Bearded Lady Café, epicenter of all things queer, artsy, and punk in 1990s San Francisco, and many others, thirteen total including our heckler and roadie, Sash Sunday. Two vanloads of queer performers taking off into the place we'd fled, "America." Town after town greeted us with sold-out shows, friendly strangers who clamored to cook us spaghetti dinners and meaty brunches. We drank for free and sold our work to older lesbians in Charlottesville, North Carolina; to hot bar dykes at Meow Mix in NYC; to goth girls in Houston, TX and FBI Agents in Washington, DC. Drag Queens in New Orleans, preppies in Boston, salty dogs in Provincetown, punks in Atlanta and thesbians in Greeneville. Macho slam poets in Austin and frat boys in Las Vegas. Literary folk in Buffalo and activists in Philly. Everywhere we went we found our people, and they were and were not who we thought they would be. Our country welcomed us. Incredibly, we realized that we *belonged* here. Our worlds got bigger, and we returned to San Francisco changed. At the end of that month we were able to pay twelve writers and one roadie $80 for their month of exhausting, twenty-four-hour-a-day work.

Those days feel far away from the tour I'm on today. I expect the engine in the van we're driving won't crack and die on the Alabama/Mississippi border at midnight on a Friday night, forcing us to sell it for parts and continue our trek illegally transporting eight passengers in a cargo van without seats. Probably the starter won't die, requiring me to crawl under the van and whack it with a hammer in order to turn on the van (we called that "Hammer

Time"). I am willing to bet cash money that our van won't overheat so severely that we can't actually turn it off, for fear that it will not turn back on again, circa 1998. No one will have to lead us in group van visualizations of cool snow falling on our overheated engine, or icicles dripping from the vents. If this van we are in right now were to burst into flames, the way some wires did on our 1999 tour, well, I'd be shocked. Our intrepid drivers are not having to keep their foot wrapped in a wet towel in order to withstand the heat of the gas pedal. Nope, we are in a *rental van*! A long, black passenger van we rent from a company that rents vans mainly to bands, and who name each of their vans after a female musician. We're driving in Harriet, but we can't figure out who Harriet is named after so we've been calling her Elvira.

When we pull into town tonight, we have a place to stay. Not like in the 1990s, when I would shout into the mic at the close of the show, Hey, can anyone put us up for the night? Someone always would. Once that someone was a girl who neglected to tell us her home was a very, very small apartment in some housing projects, which was already pretty crammed with ferret cages. Another time Sister Spit performers fell asleep on a stranger's futon only to be woken up at six in the morning by a couple of skinheads who'd come to repossess their sleeping furniture. In Tucson, a performer slept in a claw-foot bathtub. It was the coolest spot in the house. We slept in bunks on women's land in the south, no electricity, chiggers in the grass and dyke-biting-pike in the lake we swam in.

Hold on — Dorothy Allison, sprawled out barefoot next to me in the van, has started telling a story about the time Sapphire read her poem "Wilding" and the violence of the beautiful work drove out half the audience, including Angela Davis. I tried to re-focus, but then Cassie J Sneider twisted around in the front passenger seat and asked me if there had ever been any drama on any Sister Spit tours, and I was off and running for a good hour, detailing (without ever mentioning a name) the time two alcoholic members fell diabolically in love, carved hearts on each other with razors as the sun came up, and got dragged to a morning AA meeting by the tour's two sober members. Or the time our new roadie tried to run away from the tour in the middle of the night because the poet she'd kissed in a bar bathroom then kissed someone else in a bar bathroom. The heterosexual performer who had an end-of-tour meltdown, screaming "I NEED MEN AND MEAT!" after too much time spent amongst vegetarian lesbians. The diner brawl prompted by one tour member whipping a dildo from his pants and daring a circus performer we'd befriended to fellate it. A rogue Catholic in the back of the room (this was in Boston) was violently offended and started menacing us all, so I jumped into action and hurled a jar of Grey Poupon at his head, sparking rather than quelling a raging fight.

Then Dorothy asked if there had been any *romantic* dramas on Sister Spit, and I detailed the hook-ups and break-ups the tour had inspired (ten break-ups have happened on the road, plus eight hook-ups, two resulting in marriages and then subsequent divorces). I finally shut up and tried to turn back to the task at hand, only to be distracted by Brontez Purnell talking about his father back in Alabama freaking out on him for not owning land: "How are you going to get beans? You're going to go on some white man's land and they're going to kill you!" And Brontez back in Oakland, going, "Huh? I get my beans at the grocery store."

I started Sister Spit because I wanted to go on a massive roadtrip, and I don't drive. I started Sister Spit because I had a vision of a group slumber party with all the most interesting people I've met. I started Sister Spit because I was frustrated that all my friends were wild geniuses and the rest of the world didn't seem to know this. And the bonding in the van, the thrill of a new city every night, and the true joy and wonder on our audience's faces as they behold their new favorite performers and their concept of what is possible in life gets cracked open a little wider — all these things make me keep doing Sister Spit every year.

Inside this book you will see the wild make-up of a Sister Spit tour, the way everyone is so singular yet strongly linked by — what? A shared political outlook? Maybe. Queerness? Usually, but not always. Feminism? Sure, but that doesn't always look like what you think it should. A dedication to their work? Certainly, but it is something else that brings these different people together and make them work as a whole, a certain Sister Spit *je ne sais quoi*. I know it when I hear it, it makes my pulse race a bit and I start yearning to hang out at a truck stop with the person. Many but not all of them are in here, people who joined Sister Spit on our maiden voyage in 1997 to people who are out in the hotel lobby right now, drinking coffee before we get in the van and head off to our next university workshop. Fifteen years of work are in this book — classics that people read on the road, and new stuff that shows you where they're at now. Tour diaries that hilariously detail what the culture we create on the road is like. I never went to college, but it seems the bonds we make in the van are sort of like that, the sort of friendships that come out of sharing a focused, exhilarating, grueling moment in time. I hope I am still doing this when I am a very old person. And I hope all of you will be there at our shows, cheering us on.

Michelle Tea
2012

SISTER SPIT

Star

Samuel Topiary

I am the star of your Hollywood Lesbian Fantasy Movie.
I am cold and untouchable, beautiful beyond your wildest
    dreams,
I am the star of your Hollywood Lesbian Fantasy Movie.

Dangerously educated, smart like a whip,
    I am cracking against your stupid male skull,
    I am beating you out of your high paying job,
    I am stealing your beautiful wife.
    I am your fantasy, I am the star.

I am scratching out your eyes, I am slapping your face,
    I am ripping you apart with an ice-pick.
    I am shooting you down,
    I am killing you with kindness,
    screwing up your perfect life,
    seducing your neighbor's wife.

I am your fantasy,
    I am the star.
    I am your Hollywood Fantasy star.

I am fucking you over, you privileged suburban man,
    I am making you obsolete,
    I am stealing your children,
    changing your laws,
    strapping one on,
    giving you strife. . . .
    I am fucking your wife
    I am fucking your wife
    I am fucking your wife
    I am fucking your wife.
    I am your fantasy.

I am the star. . . .
    I am your Hollywood fantasy star,
    I am your Hollywood Lesbian Fantasy Movie star.

My Life in Ink

Cooper Lee Bombardier

When I was eleven years old, I drew tattoos in thick pencil on this shiny-surfaced paper recycled from my father's work, and sold the little hearts and anchors for a nickel to kids at school. I was a shitty capitalist even then, and a real softy when a kid wanted one of my tattoos but didn't have the cash. To apply my tattoos all a kid had to do was lick their skin, stick the tiny drawing graphite-side down, and press for a count of three. I didn't make much money but soon half the children in my grade were running through the school hallways with smudgy ships, dragons, and unicorns blackening their skinny forearms.

My first tattoo was a crappy ankh on my right pinky finger — I did it myself with a safety pin and ink from one of my radiograph pens. It was 1987 and I was in art school, blossoming into an aquanetted deathy punk-rock wonder. I was all about the *Egyptian Book of the Dead* and found joy in anything angry or morbid. Really, I was desperate to find a way to live inside my own skin, hang curtains and call it home, perhaps finding a way to exist in this world. Covering myself with tattoos seemed like a good start.

I was the first of my various circles of friends to begin to be tattooed. During my first year at MassArt, an older and spectacular goth girl named Patti Day told me she was getting tattooed. Tattooing was illegal in Massachusetts in 1987, an enforcement that lasted from the late 1960s until the turn of the century. *Where, with who? I desperately wanted to know, Because I want tattoos!* Patti invited me to her apartment in Allston, and soon after my arrival a dapper, biker-looking guy knocked on the door. He carried two small suitcases, and made some shy small talk in a calm, quiet voice. His name was Mark. He unpacked his equipment with nimble swiftness and was soon stepping on his pedal, revving his tattoo gun like a racecar at a stoplight, examining the needle-bar as it flicked in and out of the tip of the filler tube like a hummingbird's tongue. He had drugstore reading glasses far down on his nose like a grandmother, which managed to only make him look even more cool and tough rather than frumpy. He sat up and glanced from me to Patti, *OK. Who's first.* No turning back now.

Mark gave me two tattoos in Patti's flat that evening. I also got Mark's business card, and shortly after started scheduling him for tattoo parties at my Mission Hill flat. My friends would come up to Boston from the South Shore on the Red Line T train. Mark would arrive looking handsome and biker tough with his little cases, and tattoo six or eight of us in an evening. I got to know my underground tattoo artist well enough to have actual conversation with him, hear him laugh. We were kids, getting silly things etched onto us forever as if there would never be a tomorrow, a tomorrow where you might want to cover up that Eye of Horus. If he thought we were goofy, he was gracious enough to never let on. He carried a solemn manner of decorum and he would only accept a cold beer from us after the last person was bandaged up, very professional. Years later I discovered photos of Mark in Nan Goldin's book, *The Ballad of Sexual Dependency*, from 1978 — a decade before I started getting tattoos from him. In the Nan Goldin pictures he looks skinny, shining with sweat and drugs, big eyed and young. A bloody-bandaged tattoo on his thin hip. I remember wishing I still had a way to contact him. I had so many questions.

In 1990 I got a girlfriend who was a tattoo artist — and not a good one. Maybe just an okay one. She tried to teach me how to tattoo but she didn't have the patience. Also, I don't think she knew enough herself to impart instruction to anyone else. She once tore the gun out of my hands while I was working on her leg. Impatient and hot-headed, she finished it herself, grumbling like I was an idiot.

When I moved to San Francisco in 1993, there was an abundance of great artists from whom to get tattooed. I promptly got a sacred heart in memory of my brother from the legendary Freddie Corbin. I began to frequent Ed Hardy's shop in North Beach — long before his name started blowing up on soap bottles and lighters at Walgreens.

In those early days of my SF tenure, I lived at the renowned 122 Webster Street House in the Lower Haight, home of the Webster Street Witches. One day I answered a knock at my door — I figured it was one of the local crack aficionados wanting to borrow matches, but to my surprise there were two ethereal girls swaying on my stoop and holding hands. *We heard you did tattoos will you give us tattoos?* They asked with nary a comma, like Children of the Corn or something. I eyeballed them hard. One was short and dark haired with a croaking amphibian voice and a huge septum piercing glimmering above a wispy mustache and slight beard. All of her clothes were the same color brown as her eyes, hair, and beard. The other girl was tall and ghosty in bleached hair and a cream colored Victorian gown that was street-sooty and tattered at the hem. They wore a vegan pallor that made the two of them seem to be a sepia-tone tintype photograph come to life. They swayed back and forth slightly as if to a breeze or unheard music, but my guess was really heroin. *I am not a tattoo artist you guys. Sorry.* They just stared at me harder in their close, narcotic way. *Will you give us tattoos anyway?* They implored. *No, guys, I'm sorry.* Which felt difficult to say during a time of my life where I seemed to be saying *YES* to everything else.

But not long after, 1994 or something, there I was in that same house, drinking cold beers with Shanna Banana, giving each other jailhouse tattoos — sewing needles grouped in a tight bundle with cotton thread, and Waterman India ink blobbed into an upturned bottle cap. We watched *The Decline of Western Civilization* on VHS and gave each other tattoos that read "Sister" to the sounds of the Germs and X.

Just a couple of years later I landed an actual tattoo apprenticeship at Black and Blue, next door to Red Dora's Bearded Lady. This was an amazing and generous opportunity that I completely squandered; not out of laziness, but from immaturity maybe, and definitely from doing too much. I swirled in some kind of energetic fugue state of grief, terrified of ever spending two minutes alone with myself. When I took the apprenticeship I was also in a band, Dirt Bike Gang; I created a series of huge paintings, and laborious hand-drawn band posters; I landed several art shows, wrote furiously and performed often — I was at a creative zenith. And I worked three jobs, took up smoking, slept with just about *everyone*, attempted to drown my grief in booze, and was housing my dear friend Atom in my bedroom for several months. In the spirit of saying *YES* to everything, I took on a tattoo apprenticeship — a serious endeavor that requires commitment, responsibility, and focus, things that I couldn't seem to access in my life. So for a few months I soldered lots of tattoo needles onto holder bars, made signs for the shop, and flirted with the hot girls who came in to a dyke-owned tattoo shop to be inked up. Then I left in the summer to go on tour with Sister Spit — the first tour, in 1997.

I can't even say how it started, who wanted me to do it first. I tattooed about half our crew with jailhouse-style (the trendy parlance these days is "stick 'n' poke") commemorative tour tattoos — scraggly stars with uneven arms like baby starfish, or a star with the initials O and K on either side to salute our beloved OK Van (R.I.P.). One had a little trail of stardust like a shooting star — it may have been to camouflage a mistake, and a couple of them came out not half bad! I gave them in bars and on a picnic table at a Texas anarchist compound. I gave them in living rooms in Buffalo. I wanted mine on my hand, but I couldn't bear to do a lumpy star on my own hand so triple Virgo and future Sister Spit tour member Stanya gave me a lovely little star on the web of my right hand in Williamsburg. I could not and would not vouch for the quality of my work. I would agree to do it if the person promised that they were okay with being possibly quite bummed about the result. It was a bit of a surprise that others wanted their tour tattoos after seeing the first or second. They were shaky and uneven but weirdly full of heart. Actually, I don't know anyone, myself included, who gets homemade tattoos with sewing needles and India ink because they want an excellent tattoo. It is about an immediacy, an intimacy, an indelible souvenir of a time and of a place that you will never return to as you sail forth in your life's own ocean. It is about a connection, a reminder, a friendship, an adventure. You can look at your scraggly little star and remember: *I was there.*

Sister Spit 2011 Tour Diary

Blake Nelson

DAY ONE:

The Sister Spit tour is underway. First stop last night was Mills College, which I have no pictures of, because I didn't bring my stupid camera because I brought a FLIP camera instead because everyone keeps telling me that everyone loves video but I don't, because I don't have time to look at it, and I especially don't have time to film it.

Anyway, so we rolled into Mills and asked directions from some super-cute hipster girls (who were hanging around the parking lot like Fashion Juvenile Delinquents). We got to the student center which was a beautiful dark wooded room, the likes of which you don't even notice when you're a student but later in life you think: wasn't I supposed to end up in beautiful dark wooded rooms? What happened to me?

Then we ate. In the cafeteria I couldn't figure out how to order because I don't know anything about food, and colleges have gotten pretty sophisticated about that stuff. Really. I couldn't figure out how to order SPAGHETTI with red sauce.

Note to college kids: it's kind of up to you to save the world from Global Self-Destruction, so maybe a little less time foodying and a little more time reinventing human society? Thank you.

So then the show commenced and it was the first time the eight performers all got to see exactly what the others did. It was great. People were GOOD. And FUNNY. I was laughing my ass off the whole time!!

The room was packed. And it was a big room. This is apparently normal for Sister Spit.

Afterward, we loaded out and drove back over the Bay Bridge, chatting happily and watching San Francisco glitter beneath us as we crossed back into "The City" as I seem to recall Bay Area people call downtown.

Then I got to wake up this morning in the lower Haight, surrounded by Michelle Tea's amazing book collection and found the *Adderall Diaries* which I have been meaning to read for ages and so spent the morning with that.

To hell with beautiful dark wooded rooms. I have a dream life now!

DAY TWO:

Thanks to a generous grant from someone, Sister Spit Tour hit San Jose for the first time in its history. We were told this might be a smaller than usual turnout, but it wasn't that bad. Also the art space we were in had a show up by Jamie Hernandez of LOVE AND ROCKETS fame that was fun to look at.

Afterward we cruised the deserted streets of San Jose, which is apparently unpopulated for the most part. An interesting concept for a city: no people. We found a VOODOO DONUTS rip off called PSYCHO DONUTS, or maybe it's vice versa, where I had a joke donut of some sort which I did not particularly enjoy.

Oh well, another day, another ten dollar per diem.

DAY THREE:

Tonight we played the awesome, super adorable ROCK PAPER SCISSORS collective in Oakland.

When I enter places like this I feel like I am entering a humble monastery of perfect "girl" essence. They had sewing machines and fabric and textures and everything is free or shared and everyone present is (or becomes upon entering) super gentle and kind and polite and nurturing.

I always feel like I am some sort of crude peasant in the face of such cultural sublimity and generosity, and I seem always in such places to have a little moment of humility of: "wow, look where I am."

There was a whole upstairs with a shockingly huge library of zines including my favorite issue of COMETBUS where he discusses the ways in which Portland (my hometown) resembles a bad mood. . . . What was I thinking not doing some serious Cometbus reading before I even came down to the Bay Area? Someday there will be high schools in the East Bay named COMETBUS. Not in our lifetime maybe . . . but someday . . .

But I digress. ROCK PAPER SCISSORS was great and it was of course, packed with cute Sister Spit fans piled up on the staircase, sitting on the floor, packed on the couch. Really a great audience. Myriam "Gerbz" Gurba was especially good tonight. I had a little panic about what I was going to read, I ended up reading from *Girl*. I babbled stupidly about skinheads during my introduction. Like what is the contemporary equivalent? Is there any subculture that is scary and bullyish like that now? The girls looked at me funny.

Later that night, back in SF, I helped load some PA equipment into the sex club which had nicely lent it to us. That was fun for me, having never walked through the showers of a gay sex club carrying a PA speaker before. Ah, the bucket list slowly fills!

DAY FOUR:

On DAY 4, we played the Echo nightclub in LA. Weird to arrive in a city that I supposedly live in but which looked very alien and new to me. LA has such a strange otherworldly vibe to it. I still don't understand it. I am so not a Californian . . .

BUT THE SHOW. IT WAS GREAT. The other Spit veterans said it was the best L.A. show Sister Spit has ever done, and it did indeed rock. There were some great guest performers, Raquel Gutierrez and Amber Benson, plus the core group of us were all especially good for some reason.

The next day we cruised up to Sacramento in an unbelievable monsoon, where a theater full of locals braved the weather and came out to see us. So impressive how Sister Spit draws no matter what. The place was nearly full! And like trees were being uprooted, so bad was the storm.

I read from *Destroy All Cars* and cracked myself up, being a little giddy from the long van ride, but the crowd seemed to enjoy my lack of professionalism. A neat trick was thus learned: laugh at your own jokes and other people — if they don't laugh — will at least wonder what the fuck is your problem.

We bailed out of The Sac and cruised home in the wee hours of the night. Amos Mac had the genius idea to get a hot chocolate out of a rest area vending machine. Vending Machine Hot Chocolate is the best!!!!

Tonight, we did the Elbo Room in the mission. This is where Lauren Cerand and I saw our first Sister Spit show last year, and it KILLED. Not so much tonight. We were okay. Medium show I thought. There was all this press there, and millions of friends, easy to get distracted. Ali and I hid in the dressing room and said funny things to each other. Ali Liebegott might be the funniest person I have ever physically sat next to.

DAY NINE:

Down to L.A. again, to Pasadena City College. It is becoming clear there is no predicting which gigs are going to be amazing and which are going to be merely solid and fun.

At PCC we were late. We called ahead to tell them and they were deeply worried about us. We got the idea right then that this was going to be a special show.

As we drove around Pasadena looking for the proper parking lot, we spotted some queer students jumping up and down at the corner and waving at us. Then they ran down the sidewalk wildly pointing us into the proper parking lot, sacrificing themselves for the good of the others, since now they would have to run all the way back to the student center. It was a profound act of personal bravery and selflessness.

Inside the PCC crowd was huge to bursting. They were SO EX-CITED to have us there. They were freaking the fuck out. We were all deeply moved by their total commitment to Sister Spit.

We then hit USC the next night, it was a terrible rain storm which I think dampened the crowd a bit, also it was a huge room so despite having a respectable turnout it felt a little diffuse.

I did have a fun moment asking a USC student what the essential nature of USC was and without blinking she offered something like: "It's a school of privileged entitled white kids spending four years doing coke on their parent's credit cards." I love it when people say stuff like that. I hated everything when I was in college. Including my college.

The following afternoon we went back to PCC to hang with the Queer Alliance which I skipped, which was a total mistake as the PCC kids were just so into shit and I should have known not to miss this but I did but they gave me one of their awesome t-shirts anyway.

Then we drove to Long Beach and checked into the Queen Mary and had a great gig at a coffee shop in Long Beach where Gerbz is from and so she had a big crowd and sold a million of her cool new chapbooks that Kevin Sampsell sent down from Portland. (I love it when my old friends are the publishers of my new friends. We're all one big family it turns out, unlike what I thought in college when I thought the world was evil, and my only chance for survival was to destroy everything.)

The Long Beach gig was in a great homey coffee-shop that was awesome and PACKED and everyone sold a lot of crap at the merch table.

Kirk Read read his response to Myriam Gurba's wildly popular new piece: "I Would Be a Better Lesbian If:" with his own: "I Would Be a Better Queer if:" Kirk often writes amazing poems on the spot, and performs them like ten minutes later. It is fun to see him curled up in some corner, furiously pounding something out at the last second.

Later, some *Girl* fans cornered me and got me to sign a VERY OLD copy of *Girl*. "I've read it many, many times," the fan said. The cover was literally about to fall off. That was really nice.

Then a night of hi jinks running around the Queen Mary which was great retro fun and seriously impressive as a physical object. We build miraculously tiny things now, (microchips or whatever), in those days they built miraculously HUGE things.

DAY ELEVEN:

So we survived Santa Cruz but just barely. Naturally, some raver, Satan-worshipping, acid-damaged twenty-somethings ended up in our hotel, THE TORCHLITE, so there was some problems there. Nothing Kirk Read couldn't handle, though. When the confrontation escalated, he reduced their leader to a trembling puddle of wussiness, in one of the most awesome verbal takedowns I have ever seen in my life.

So then we packed up our crap and got the hell out of there and went to beautiful Arcata, home of Humboldt State College, where we performed for a movie theater full of locals. This is the legendary MARIJUANA BELT part of the country. I don't know where the buckle is or where exactly the belt part goes, but Humboldt County is famous for its pot and the hotel smelled of pot and the town smelled of pot and the people we all met all appeared to be high. It was weird small-town-esque. But nice.

I started having some sort of physical reaction as we continued north toward Portland (my hometown). The cold, the damp, the rain, the sadness of the sky, I just couldn't take it and started having seasonal disorder depression almost as soon as we drove over the border. And of course whenever I see trucker-hatted, woolen-wearing older men get out of their mud-splattered pickups I think for a second it is my dad who has passed away but lives on in the black earth of the Oregon woods.

But then we did our Holocene show in Portland and it was GREAT. Packed room, as per usual. Kirk started us off dressed as an insane leopard. Everyone was killing it, as the crowd was right with us.

And then my favorite part of the night: NICOLE GEORGES! I love her stuff so much. She just IS something, she represents something, I can't say exactly what, our times, our world, Portland, whatever, and then besides doing that, her writing is so sharp and fun and dead on. The zine excerpts she did were of her doing substitute teaching and her interactions with stoner boys and bimbo high school girls were so fucking funny and right. I was in heaven. She could have gone on and on.

Now on up to legendary Olympia today. One of the fun things

about Sister Spit is it kind of sensitizes you. Like since it's mostly women, and mostly people with extra amazing radar (Michelle Tea) it makes *you* extra sensitive to subtle IN THE AIR vibrations, that you might not pick up on normally. Am I making any sense? Just to say that hitting Olympia on this tour will not be like stopping there for a cup of coffee, and the town is sort of world historic anyway, as one of the two great focal points of a certain kind of nineties youth cultural flowering, DC being the other place. Hmmmmmm. We'll see.

DAY THIRTEEN:
So we drove to Olympia and had what seemed like a week there. It rained for two days straight. It felt like Eugene. Wet. Cold. Grimy kids in the street with dogs on ropes. We stayed in a cheerful hotel called The Governor where the people all seemed to hesitate for a moment before addressing us in their cheerful hotel tones.

The show was at the Voyeur. Very nice staff. They fed us. They had cool shit on the stereo (Flipper "Sex Bomb Baby") and unrelated 80s videos playing on various broken TVs.

Audience was rain-soaked. Standing in the back of the club it felt like a not very responsive crowd but when it was my turn and I weaved my way to the microphone I found myself surrounded on all sides by a colorful carpet of floor-sitting queer kids. There was not a single open space of floor visible. Though they didn't say much, they seemed deeply in tune with us. There was a lot of love in that room. Magical even though quiet and subdued. I read from *Girl*, the relatively eventless Chapter 17 about Cybil playing soccer. Not trying for anything big really. And it totally worked. Reminds me of my band days. Some days the audience doesn't want a show, they just want the music.

Afterward sitting around in the dining area, watching the

college-aged Olympians drinking Rainer Beer. They all sport the beards, suspenders, old-timey looks of prospectors from the past. In the van we make fun of this new trend, but it is a pretty awesome look.

DAY FOURTEEN:

In Seattle, the show shaped up nicely. Hugo house was cool. Nice literary folk running things. Girl at the front desk, NOT wearing low rise jeans but some other kind that sat way high up her waist, and looked AWESOME. Not that I spend my days looking at girl's jeans or anything. But I hate low rise, always have, and am eager for the next thing.

Then the show started and we suddenly realized we had THE PERFECT AUDIENCE. Don't know why. They loved EVERYTHING WE DID. We were standing around in the back, looking at each other with bewilderment, what had we done to deserve this? Everyone KILLED. We could do no wrong. People were laughing, crying, making out, but mostly roaring with approval at anything we said or did on stage. By the time we were done people were exhausted, wrung out, high on life. The best show yet, it was called. And it was!

On the way out I was imagining what it would be like to be young and to have moved to Seattle, from Bumfuck, USA. Wearing weird clothes. Drinking great coffee. Talking about poetry and literature and hanging out at places like this. The BIG CITY! Great fun.

DAY FIFTEEN:

Riding in the van and getting bored, you start rummaging around for stuff to read . . . picked up KING KONG THEORY that one of my comrades was reading and had my mind quietly blown. It's by Virginie Despentes, a French feminist writer who is apparently famous for a book and movie she wrote called RAPE ME, which I didn't really know about.

What a great read, it never slowed down. Interesting. Funny. Compassionate thoughts on the men's side of things, reflections on her punk rock life, her rape, the weirdness of being famous as a feminist author/filmmaker and the shit storm that inevitably rained down upon her.

It also had a great rhythm, vacillating between strident manifesto, then quiet personal reflection. Kind of like Kurt Cobain stepping on and off the SUPER FUZZ pedal. Just when you don't want any more bone-crunching declarations you are suddenly hanging out with the seventeen-year-old author, going to punk shows, drinking beer. Being young and kind of out of place in the pretty girl world.

DAY SIXTEEN:

So we get to Vancouver and we're staying in this trendy hotel/theater/salon complex. A very interesting place, very Euro in its concept. The people that worked at the hotel were a little useless, but we have been spoiled recently. Still, when you're doing the hotel thing you kind of need things sometimes from the hotel people and it sucks when they're busy buying shoes on Zappos.

DAY EIGHTEEN:

Holy crap, so we show up at Bard (we're on the east coast now) and our gig is on the back porch of a barn, outside, in the freezing rain, at night, next to woods that Kirk Read immediately disappeared into. Kirk being our resident queer redneck hunter/outdoorsman, he went to study the fresh turds of various critters and varmints.

But no, it later turns out it's a garage and the gig will be *inside* it. As soon as someone *unlocks* it. Which nobody did for an hour. We're all like, okay, this is cool, as we step through the mud in our useless California shoe wear. (I'm wearing white vans . . . good call!)

So they open it up and we set up our crap and things are

turning out a little more like we planned. Still, all of this is running way behind schedule so that weird artsy Bard kids start appearing and disappearing and wandering around. One awesome girl had an eye catching KAREN O haircut and the weirdest coolest face ever. I should have tried to chat with her but why? They're just college kids. You talk to them and there just isn't anything there yet.

I mention this girls' haircuts because I think that Yeah Yeah Yeah's were formed at Bard, and also because HAIRCUTS MATTER. A cool haircut by a single audience member makes a "medium" gig into a "good" gig. And this girl had a cute dress too. She looked great. WEAR COOL CLOTHES PEOPLE. Give back.

So we drove the next day to Colby Sawyer College in New Hampshire and had another subdued gig which was nevertheless fun and we went ape-shit during our free meal in the college cafeteria in any event. I had ALL the dinner options. Meatloaf. Fettuccine. Hamburger. And just kept eating until I couldn't move because I LOVE INSTITUTIONAL FOOD OF ANY KIND. Ali Liebegott was with me on this.

During the show, I read a bit of *Recovery Road* which went well though I started to get choked up reading about the tragic love of Maddie and Stewart. I almost started crying!!! On Stage!!!! You get a little raw emotionally on the road.

And Michelle read a great piece about rad-ass teenagers from her book *Rose of No Man's Land* which I love hearing from. I love all the books people have been reading from. Everyone on the tour is a great writer, which makes it fun no matter what the circumstances or varying crowds.

DAY TWENTY-THREE:
At Colby Sawyer College, after the show, we hung out with some co-eds from there who told us about school and what they were

studying. There were several Women's Studies majors and they were telling us about feminism and rape culture as if we'd perhaps never heard of them.

So the next night I decided to bust out my old *Details* article: "How To Date A Feminist" at the U Mass show. I have never read this piece in public. It was considered pretty controversial in the nineties when it came out, making gentle fun both of doctrinaire feminism, and the kind of dumb men's/women's glossy magazine articles. Anyway, it went over big, and got a lot of laughs and though it was clearly dated in some of its references, ("compliment her Doc Martins") pretty much all the points were still pretty valid. "Almost all smart women are feminists, but not all feminists are smart."

The rest of the show was great, including the finale in which a witch put a spell on all of us. And the best part: there were like 500 people there. We filled an entire BALLROOM!!

The next day we went to Emily Dickenson's house. When the tour guide asked if any of us were fans of Emily Dickenson, Ali Liebegott pulled up her shirt sleeve and showed the woman her full-arm tattoo of Ms. Dickenson's portrait. The guide woman — thus energized — gave us a great tour, full of gossip and conjecture and hearsay. And we got to see Emily's white dress, goddesslike and ethereal.

DAY TWENTY-EIGHT:
A local spoken word group opened the show at Louisville. They were called S.H.E. and it was interesting to see them, because it made me realize how being on the tour had honed our skills. Not that the S.H.E. kids weren't good, they just weren't as individualized as we had become. But a great experience for them I'm sure and for us to see what the younger kids were thinking about and writing about.

After the show, we went to a girl named Lex's house and ka-raoked and were invited to hot tub with some people in their un-derwear, which none of us managed to do. They were super nice though and their house was filled with the signifiers of indie queer-ness: cool Bratmobile poster. Joy Division poster. Fever Ray on the stereo. Tons of interesting books to look at. Generally I'm finding college kids to be a bit more clueless than I expected but the Louis-ville people seemed pretty awesome.

Also Louisville the town kicked ass, being older than I expect-ed and having a real sense of character and history. We wondered among ourselves: what would it be like to move to Louisville? Ali did an impromptu performance piece of what exactly such a move would turn into, which was brilliant and true and had us all crack-ing up.

We ended up that night in a gross rooming-house situation and Beth Pickens, our road manager, got us out of there and into a super nice old hotel downtown for super cheap. The place was amazing and had WEIRDLY NICE ECCENTRIC people working there which is the mark of greatness as far as I'm concerned when it comes to hotels.

I started saying a couple years ago that as you get older and you don't want to go to clubs anymore, you will go to hotels to meet people and hang out. I LOVE HOTELS. I should have stayed in my band. I would have got all the hotels I wanted.

Anyway, so now we are in a gross Super 8 on the freeway by Bloomington, Indiana which was FRAT PARTYING out all around us. Nice though to be in the Midwest. My dad is from Iowa and I dress just like him, and so when I'm in the Midwest, I look around and see millions of versions of myself. American Prep.

DAY THIRTY-ONE:

MARYS! We only have two more dates on the tour!!! Everyone is so sad!! It's been SO FRICKIN' FUN!!

"Mary," by the way, is what everyone calls each other in the van.

One can be addressed as "Mary." "Can you hand me those cheese balls, Mary?"

One can express things to the Gods in the form of Mary. "Mary, is it ever going to stop raining?"

And one can simply say the word to oneself as a kind of protection from all human trials and tribulations. "Mary!"

Probably this is some ancient and well known gay slang that every gay person in the world knows about. But it was new and fresh to me.

So we left Bloomington and drove up to Ann Arbor where we had PHOEBE GLOECKNER as a guest performer!! MARY!! We are all INSANE fans of hers. The gig was weirdly not packed — we are spoiled — but it didn't matter and created a loose fun atmosphere which I like.

Phoebe went on last and told us about her new project and she was a little bit nervous but spoke interestingly about her life as an artist. It was more like a big conversation really, all of us chirping in, asking questions, etc. And then we had a great dinner after, paid for by the awesome gay bookstore COMMON LANGUAGE who helped put on the show.

Then back to one of the less nice hotels, but comfy for us as we all have gotten used to each other and don't mind stepping over each other's underwear on the way to the bathroom, or getting tangled up in MariNaomi's sleeping bag (not like camping, an actual anti-allergen body bag), or getting rolled over on in our sleep. Or snored upon (Kirk).

In Milwaukee, I read a piece about hanging with Courtney Love in Portland when I was a wee little Portland scenester. I thought the local queer kids might notice who I was reading about but they didn't seem to, having missed the whole Kurt and Courtney era. And probably not caring anyway, despite the HOLE-worship still practiced by Tavi and her ilk.

Then it was back into the van and onto Minneapolis, home of F. Scott Fitzgerald and Garrison Keillor. Mostly I think of it through F. Scott's eyes though, but of course the world of rich kids riding around in motorboats on the lake is not anywhere I am going to be. Isn't that always the case? You go to some famous spot that is so alive in your mind only to realize, Truman Capote's New York is not in Central Park, it's up there, in those penthouses, which you can't get to. That's why people love it so much. Inaccessible.

We did get to see a little bit of rich kid cool at Seward's Café though, which is the trendy foodie hipster restaurant that Sister Spit frequents on all trips to the Twin Cities. I don't go to such places usually, but I have to get over that because this place was full of such interesting people, the Volvo/Oberlin/Crafter crowd. I couldn't get enough. Beautiful young women in their Chic Minnesota Woolens. MARY! I was dying with envy and falling in love with everyone. Why do I have such little interaction with this world? So nice. So cultured. So FOODIE FRIENDLY. Why can't I be a normal person!!?? I want to be like these people. Saturday brunch with friends! Everyone equal and happy and well adjusted and having good jobs and having just graduated from excellent liberal arts colleges. Oh I am such a mess compared to these people. But perhaps I am comparing "my insides to their outsides" which is never recommended.

Oh yeah, the gig. We sold out Bryant Park Theater, or whatever it was, in the Uptown section of Minneapolis. We packed it. Kicked it. KILLED IT. We were great. The people loved us. Then we hung out all night until the wee hours. Kirk Read and I bowled. More beautiful kids, hanging out, on dates, with friends, smoking cigarettes outside the club in their $400 Marmot down coats. Maybe F. Scott's dreams are still alive here. Despite the strange feeling at times that no matter how hard we row, "We are boats against the current, borne back ceaselessly into the past."

DAY THIRTY-FOUR:

Heading south again, trying to escape the snow and the bleakness, though I will forever hope to return to Minneapolis again to revisit the Seward Café because I think it changed my life. I think from now on I am going to become a partial foodie just because I realize that foodies are the most interesting diners, and I'll put up with anything for good people watching.

And as Michelle Tea said about several things over the course of the trip: "You don't want to be on the wrong side of History" meaning your little jealous corrupted brain full of prejudices and preconceived notions and what not, cannot always be trusted. So my anti-foodie-ism is now officially retired.

Later, we land in Madison. The space is small, a cool little collective, sort of grungy and Portland-esque. All her normal staff was ill so poor Bessie, who ran the place, had to do everything herself, including setting up the chairs which I re-spaced for her because people often don't know the secret to setting up chairs is SPACING. Nothing worse than getting stuck in a chair with no room in front of you.

So we wandered around and then drove to this super comfort food diner called Monty's that was queer friendly, or at least had a queer waiter, and a highly eclectic menu. We were served uneatable volumes of food and then stumbled out of there late and rushed back to the space and had that wonderful Sister Spit sensation of half forgetting where you are and what you're doing and walking into the gig and finding A TOTALLY PACKED HOUSE. As a writer and goer to of writer things I have never seen anything literary consistently PACK THE SPACES like SS.

We went on. We killed. The standing room only crowd gave us a standing ovation!!!

Afterward I met some YA people, which didn't happen as much as I'd hoped. That was fun. And some other fans. I never quite got the hang of hanging out after the show, I often hid in the back room, but whenever I did, I always seemed to find several fans milling around. *Girl*, especially, lives on, which is so cool, and so flattering.

The next afternoon was our final show in Chicago. Things started slow as we all stood outside in the freezing cold waiting for the SUBTERRANEAN CLUB to open. This was in trendy Wicker Park. Michelle was shaking with cold. They let us in finally. Things looked bad at first and there was a big blow up with some club people. But everything got done, as happens.

So then the show. We KILLED. AGAIN. It was great. I read the final scene in RECOVERY ROAD where Maddie tries to talk to a relapsed junkie Stewart — her one true love — and I CRIED !!!!!!!

Well I didn't actually shed tears but I kept having to step away from the mike and re-compose myself. I finally told the audience: "I'm sorry. I'm a cryer." I don't know if they were won over by that. The piece totally worked though. I achieved that great thing of total silence from the crowd which is hard to do in a bar. But that scene is so heartbreaking. Anyway, so that was the end of the tour and the end of the book and everything kind of wrapped up nicely.

I am so glad I went on this tour. It was so fun and so interesting in so many ways. And I will never forget my crew!!!! What a great time. I am sad it's over but I feel exhausted in a good way, in the best way. I LEFT EVERYTHING I HAD OUT THERE!!! Awesome!

February 13, 1982

Eileen Myles

Time passes. That's for sure. It's the nightmare of having what you want that I'm interested in today. I had a book party five years ago. It took place in New York where I live and it was the beginning of the end for me.

I'm a very different person today. Bill's coming over to build shelves in the kitchen. Things have a slow progression, kind of a pleasant listiness. A big part of my list is the past. I went over to Rose's to plan the book party. Power Mad Press, which was Barbara, was publishing my book. Barbara lived with Rose in a loft and that's where we were going to have the party. Rose is an astrologer. She pointed to February 13th on her calendar. It's got to be this date, she said. Absolutely. But why, I asked. A lot of things will converge for you on this date. Your Mars, a lot of your aspects . . . I don't know how to explain it, but this is YOU. Maybe you don't want your party to be such an intense experience. It could be a lot quieter. It depends on what you want. Rose was like a lawyer, or a salesman. You never knew if she was making this stuff up — if she really had her finger on the pulsation of the orbs and if she did, I mean, if she really had the power, was she on my side.

I watched the way she played with her cats. What if she was just very powerful and intuitive, but to her we were all just cats. It was an interesting place to be and I decided to go with her suggestion.

I made a very nice white on black invitation. Mostly the party was publicized by word of mouth. I bought some cocaine. I was a very down and out person. Sort of a beer drinker, really. The kind of person who always had diet pills in her faded jean pockets. My main concern really was that I didn't get so drunk that I fell down or turned it into an embarrassing night in some way. It was an early evening event. I had slept with this girl who was a musician and who I was currently in love with. She left around noon, left me to my cigarettes, and a nice foggy musing upon my pink floral sheets and the birds outside my window and the slender branches of the trees. I have an old cemetery outside my window and I felt like Keats in the 1800s or something. I could feel the nervousness rising in me like some kind of strange spring, inside and out. The winter had a way to go, but there's always days in February when you forget that. For me to put down one hundred dollars for cocaine was something, but all in service of this wonderful amazing day — the long-awaited book and of course my new life.

I suppose I had the typical horror of what if nobody shows up. I went over to the loft relatively early and I know I was full of the deep calm of one who is in a total panic. I smoked significant cigarettes. The whole thing wasn't very professional. We didn't even know we could sell books. We had maybe twenty available copies. The rest of the books were there in the loft but a couple of things were missing from them. One was the name of the photographer who did the photos front and back. Irene Young would be pissed if she didn't get credit so we had a stamp made and dutifully stamped her name in red ink on the credit page.

The other thing missing from the book was a whole stanza, the last stanza of a poem called "New York." Here's the stanza:

Then entering the subway, pushing through
the crowds at 34th, I saw a
baby sucking desperately on its bottle
tears streaming down its tat dark face.
As it sat in its carriage. It stopped me,
I turned, examined some flowers
for sale, cloth on silky green leaves
mounted on a comb. I plucked
up a black one, a black rose, paid the
guy a dollar. I love it.

I'm softly fingering the petals on the
subway home, it is so artificial
so dark and so beautiful.

I thought "it is so artificial / so dark and so beautiful" referred to New York. Now it strikes me that I was talking about my life. Line four should read "fat dark face," not "tat."

So what happened once the party got going was that as people wanted copies of the book I had to go into the back room and stamp "Irene Young" and the final stanza of "New York" into each copy. My book was called *A Fresh Young Voice From the Plains*. I had always figured if I had a book I would want my face all over it. The experience was like television. Every book hanging off the end of someone else's hand was like another tiny monitor. As more and more people began to flow in it meant that that many more pictures were bobbing around the room. What a horror. Particularly in relation to the people I didn't know. They would look down at their book and then up at me. Oh, it's you. Here it was a big moment in my life and to them it was just another party. I began to join that group. Some beer, some coke. Some people you know. I would go in the back and people would offer me some coke and then I would offer mine to other people. People seemed surprised that I had my own coke. Of course. It's my party. It's a self-serving event.

Allen Ginsberg asked me to sign his book. I must've stood there for five minutes drawing a complete blank. Hi Allen, from one howl to another. Dear Allen I'm glad you think I'm a poet. Love, Eileen. I'm the only woman you like, right Allen? Only the craziest thoughts passed through my mind. Finally he started getting embarrassed. Just sign it. Come by and write something better when you think of it. I scrawled something. I forget what it was.

I was "The Fresh Young Voice from the Plains." I felt so foolish signing books. "Mark, you're going to kill yourself if you keep drinking the way you do. Me too. Eileen." The wrong lines kept flashing through my mind. In David's I wrote: David, I just wrote something really horrible in someone's book. People I didn't know wanted copies and I would put them off and they'd offer money, go "C'mon, I'll pay for it." At the end my pants were full of these wrinkled dollar bills. It made me feel kind of sleazy, through Barbara was the most laissez-faire publisher ever and I'm sure she didn't give a shit.

Rene was skipping around. That made it a real party. He was talking to Ted who was there in his dark blue short sleeve shirt. Ted found my discomfort so amusing. How're you doing, *Eileen?* He put this faggy little turn on "Eileen," like it was a made-up name, something I'm pretending to be. It sounded right. It sure amused Rene who kept telling me how fabulous my book party was in a way which made me wonder if this wasn't the worst party of all time.

The girl musician was blowing her saxophone in the middle room with all her musician friends who were taking this party as an opportunity to play or impress each other or whatever musicians do. She seemed to think they wouldn't let her in on all their men things if they knew she was a "lezzy" so I could barely get a hello out of her.

My couple didn't come. I sort of moved in on this couple of poets that winter. I liked him, but I adored her and that was falling apart around this time, but at least they could come to my book party. I used to wear a Timex watch and she was always asking me what time it was. I planned to give her a watch of her own at the party but she didn't come. Suddenly I had this extra watch. I had also guiltily bought him a purple striped tie. What was I going to do with that tie. I asked my sister to hold the stuff in her bag. She wound up going back to Boston with the watch and the tie and eventually they came back in the mail. Then I gave Mark Breeding the watch. The tie just hung out with my other ties for a few years until I realized I didn't wear ties.

Yeah, my sister from Boston came to the party. A representative of the Myleses from Boston. Unfortunately, she had just broken up with her boyfriend the night before. She thought the trip would be good for her, a distraction. People always think that until they get a few drinks in them.

I wore a striped boat-neck shirt. There was a poem in my book about a dog named Skuppy who sailed the seven seas and lived in his own private boat. I secretly knew that I was a dog who lived in a boat. The floors in my apartment had a definite slant and the trees outside would get going in the wind and I was always kind of staggering around so it was a pretty natural image to grab onto. Vickie picked up on it and greeted me: Hey Skuppy! I barked. She had the same shirt on. Mark told me he had also considered buying the shirt and would have worn it as well. I guess it was 1982 and it was an obvious shirt to have that year.

Chassler, who also lived in the loft, had two kids from his last marriage. They were great, they were sort of the pets of the loft. These kids always had some toy that we were all playing with. Nora had a parrot on a stick. You could make the parrot bite by moving the stick. Once my sister got a little loaded she started nipping at me with the parrot. She started aiming for the crotch a lot, and I started to get the picture that my sister was going out of control. She wasn't mixing very good and she kept turning to me for love and affection . . . and then these kind of odd sexual gestures.

It wasn't my day. Or was it? Chris showed up. She was living in Maine with Judy. She didn't look so happy and she looked like she had put on some weight. Somehow I think the experience of being in New York all of a sudden with its great frank energy was completely terrifying to her. People walk up and say things like: I don't mean to offend you . . . but you look really big. I mean, it's good. Do you do anything there? What do you do? Christine looked immediately like she was going to cry and eventually she did. Judy seemed like one of those nurse-type girlfriends. She had her arm around Chris who wouldn't look up. We gotta go, Judy smiled. But thanks a lot! Don't forget brunch tomorrow! People started asking me if I was having a good time. Are you okay?

The thing I couldn't look at was that book. On the front I stand with these crooked bangs and big bags under my eyes against the white wall of my apartment. You can see the buzzer maybe a foot and a half from my right shoulder. My face looks puffy and shapeless, fortunately I have kind of a big mouth so it sort of works. My arms look weird, though. I had been doing a lot of speed in that period of time, so I'm thin but it looks like bones with all this loose flesh tied on. The arms always look scary to me. Old. Folded across my ribs. There's other things that bother me about the front of the book, but look at the back.

Here I am lighting a cigarette, here is my can of beer on my desk. There's the typewriter. Poems all over the desk. I used to know what that big one was, but I can't remember now. And here the skin that my arms were made up of now makes up my face. I look like an old lady. It is really scary.

I had been to a million book parties since I lived in New York but mine seemed made up. I wanted to go home. There were three places to be in that loft: in the back room doing coke — it was actually most comfortable back there. It was smaller, and it had that kind of enforced closeness that feels safe in a screwed up way. But the coke made me feel more and more like one of those cubes of glass they use to create partitions with. Can I put on sunglasses? I wasn't sure.

I'd go out into the fray passing the musicians' area each time. They weren't playing music like you could dance to, it was an inner experience they seemed to be involved in. I think they were all junkies. I still could hardly get a wave out of you know who. I leaned over and said, We're all going someplace in a while, you wanna come? She nodded.

The front room was still loosely packed with drinking smoking people, oh yeah, and there were all kinds of joints circulating and for one lucky day in my life I managed to say no to them. Since I was already completely paranoid I couldn't imagine where I'd go if I smoked pot. People were beginning to leave, they were saying you want to eat with us, or we've got another party, or I've got a rehearsal, or you know me, when you get to be my age (turns up his collar) we go home when the getting's good. He raised his eyebrows. Hey Allen, wanna share a cab? The Dads are leaving I thought. This means something.

Rose's girlfriend from Chicago was in town and I was part of a troop going to Café Society, one of those part-time lesbian bars. I was bringing my sister, I was bringing the musician and I was completely depressed, but my face was frozen into a grim smile. Eileen, Rose screamed as we piled into a cab, did you have fun?

She was using the same tone she used on her cats. Yeah, it was great, Rose. Thanks a lot. Where are you going, squinted the musician. I felt like tying a rope to her leg. I was so convinced she wasn't going to stick around at all. I was right. As soon as we got inside the kind of glitter ball, tall hyacinths-in-a-vase Italian lesbian disco environment I could see her squirming free. I sighed. I hate disco, she said. You can't tell me you like this. Like? I didn't even know what that meant. Well, no, but . . . Listen, I gotta go, she said. It was that fast.

My sister seemed ready to go off. She kept putting her arm around me like . . . you know. I guess she was really upset about her boyfriend. I couldn't handle it. She kept saying sentimental things to me. She was really bombed, and I wanted to be nice and I knew she was a mess, but I really didn't want her touching me. Especially now that the musician had left. By the time we were all at the front of the bar the situation had reached its crisis. My sister had her arms around me and her head on my shoulder and I absolutely couldn't handle it. We had shared a room for seventeen years. If she wanted love and affection why couldn't she have asked then.

Everything was all confused. At the party people kept saying the musician looked like a younger version of me. I thought she looked like my sister. Lookit, I said, why don't you sit over there. Unhinging her arm from me. She held her head down and shook it grievously. The attack. You don't care about anyone but yourself. She was bombed. I could tell by the way she was shaping her words. That's it. That's the whole story. She waved her arms with a referee's gesture of closure. You don't care about anyone but yourself. All you think about is yourself, you don't even know other people are alive, you're so selfish. It's true. She doesn't care about any of you. Think she does? She doesn't. I know her, she's a phony. A fucking phony. Well, I hate you and I'm leaving. I'm going back tonight. She still held the parrot on the stick. She grabbed her suede jacket off the stool and her bag was on her shoulder. I hate you and I never want to see you again. You are so, and she broke into sobs, selfish! She ran out the door. I looked up at the faces that surrounded me. She's your sister, Eileen. Eileen, this is a very important night for you, said Rose. It counts. Should I go? I don't want to go. I was thinking: It's my night. It's my party. This isn't fair.

I caught up with Bridget on 5th Ave. and we jumped in a cab. I tried to sort of pet her. Don't touch me, she shrieked. You can't make it better now. I never want to see you again. In my apartment I watched her call the trains and discover she had just missed the last to Boston. I'll get a hotel. I will not stay here tonight. She didn't have far to go. She threw herself down on my bed and I took her boots off. In a few minutes she was out like a light.

I wanted to be anyplace but home. It was 12:30. I was sitting on my couch. On the coffee table I had my cigarettes, my little vial of coke and the red phone. And a mirror, of course. A big piece of thick broken mirror I had found in the trash. This is the picture that should have been on the book. I could see my sister's legs and skirt. It just seemed so odd to have a passed out woman on my bed. Who I know the way I know my sister. Family, great. Look at me. No one to call. My book sat on the coffee table. I felt great. I felt frozen, completely frozen in my life. It would never stop being exactly like this. I was a great poet and I would always be alone. This was my curse. I took a couple of valiums and fell asleep on the big brown velvet couch that always felt like a casket. I always heard a little voice yell my name just before I lost consciousness. I thought my death would be this way. I loved it.

from Cha-Ching!

Ali Liebegott

It was 1994, the year of bad low–blood-sugar decisions. As soon as Theo was done watching her favorite episode of TOP 25 BEST 911 EMERGENCIES she planned to leave her empty San Francisco apartment and move to New York. She sat on the cold, hardwood floor and absorbed the grave situation of a man who'd become trapped in the bottom of a garbage truck. A passerby had called 911 after hearing what sounded like "human cries" coming from out of the truck.

The police were instructed to pull over every garbage truck in a three-mile radius of the man's phone call until finally the right garbage truck was found.

A policeman approached the back with his megaphone and said, "Are you in there? Do you need help?" while two sanitation workers in bright orange vests snickered in the background smoking cigarettes.

The second time the policeman called into the garbage truck a tiny muffled voice said, "Yes, Sir. I'm down here."

The reason this was Theo's favorite episode was because the TV show never discussed how a person might find himself trapped in the bottom of a garbage truck. She knew there were only a few explanations: mental illness, drunkenness, homelessness, or a combination of the three, but by not exploring any of the options the TV show was saying, "Don't judge — we're all five decisions away from making a 911 call from the bottom of a garbage truck." And when the man was pulled gently by each of his arms from piles of oozing plastic bags, the TV show did him the additional honor of digitally blurring his face to protect his anonymity.

She snapped off the small black-and-white television but remained seated in front of it until the last bit of light fizzled into the center of the screen like a dying star. Then she yanked the thick black cord from the wall. She wasn't moving this piece of shit all the way across country. It was warm in her arms when she picked it up to carry it to the community free box. Theo climbed the two flights of stairs and opened the door that led to the roof. The cold San Francisco wind hit her squarely in the face. When she was sure she could steal no more warmth from the TV she set it down on the seat of a discarded gray office chair. There was almost never anything good in the free box, yet Theo looked at the pile daily when she passed it to smoke. With the exception of her TV it held the same things as yesterday: the disgusting office chair, some glass picture frames, worn rock-climbing shoes, and a broken, beige carpeted cat tree. All of it was trash really, but people often left trash in the free box when it wouldn't fit or they didn't want to walk the extra paces to the garbage chute.

In New York she would be a person that didn't drink or smoke or watch TV. She'd transform herself into a well-read adult, starting with the complete works of Fyodor Dostoyevsky, then move her way through biographies of famous painters. She'd always wanted to take a painting class and find out if she was secretly a brilliant artist. She'd become physically fit — get a gym membership, read *Crime and Punishment* on the stationary bicycle. Before she turned thirty she wanted to be able to go to a party and have a conversation that involved *anything* besides details from *Forensic Files* episodes.

Across the street from Theo's apartment building were some of the most dangerous housing projects in San Francisco. They had been built in the late 1960s and painted a terrible baby-shit brown. With the exception of senior citizens, residents of the housing projects were not permitted to keep dogs, but this rule was not enforced. Tenants and passersby were regularly menaced by Pit Bulls. Theo had heard the quick growl and snap of a dog and then the cry of a child once. A few minutes later an ambulance pulled up, and the boys that Theo hated who stood on the corner all day, turned their heads toward the EMTs half-interestedly. When police finally cracked the Pit Bull ring they took everything: the treadmills that the dogs were leashed to in order to train, the giant tires that hung from chains to make the dogs' jaws stronger. The beautiful, confused dogs that looked like baseball catchers with old-fashioned wire muzzles strapped over their big jaws were led out to the convoy of white Animal Care and Control Vans. Theo knew they would be euthanized as she watched them, one at a time, lunge at the dog-catcher even while muzzled. The dog-catcher was a muscular long-haired Latina butch named Denise who Theo knew from the bars. Denise did an intricate dance pushing a long pole with a wire loop at each dog. She was like a lifeguard at a city pool inserting the pole into the water for the drowning swimmer to grab onto, but to be saved the dogs needed to be calm and put their paws over the wire loop. And to be calm they needed to have had entirely different paths up until this point in their life, needed to have grown up from puppyhood not being stabbed in the ribs with screwdrivers for the sole purpose of making them mean. After all the muzzled dogs were loaded into the vans and driven away a second procession began of workers carting wheelbarrows piled high with thick, plastic bags out of the projects. It took Theo a second to realize these were the dead dogs.

Theo had watched the entire scene peeking between the mini blinds of her bedroom window. Her bedroom window was not unlike the small black and white TV in that it only got reception to a few stations. When Theo woke at 7AM she pulled her blinds up a few inches to turn on Taco Lady TV. The taco lady had already arrived two hours before in her pickup and speedily set up her mobile food cart, stretching a large bright blue plastic tarp over her truck rooftop and snapping two strong poles into place to create a little awning. She'd plugged a giant silver church percolator into a generator and arranged a tall stack of Styrofoam cups to sell coffee to people walking to the bus stop. Even though there were good cafés just a few blocks away where beautiful people sat, Theo was not willing to pay three dollars for a cup of coffee just so she could be around people in two-hundred-dollar jeans. Instead, she shuffled across the street and for a single dollar she could purchase an enormous coffee and a dry Mexican pastry. It was like having a cameo appearance on the television show she was watching. Then she'd return to her apartment, sit down on her bed, and drink her coffee while watching the neighborhood wake up. Many people shuffled over to the taco lady's truck for their morning provisions. Not everyone got a pastry. Some walked away with a tostada that was slightly larger than the tiny white paper plate it was served on. When Theo walked to work she found those tiny plates in the gutter as far as ten blocks away. The plethora of discarded plates were the taco lady's own soaring stock index. Every day but Sunday she worked from 5AM till midnight preparing meals for people in the neighborhood, opening a variety of coolers from the back of her truck when she needed ingredients for tacos and tortas. The taco lady was not getting proper rest, Theo often worried.

When she first moved into her apartment building, Theo didn't want to be like the other white people that went out of their way to walk on the opposite side of the street from the housing projects. But the regular pack of African American and Latino and Filipino boys on the corner that taunted everyone and yelled and sometimes threw empty beer bottles at passersby quickly weakened Theo's resolve. Cross the street. Look the other way. Become very involved in lighting a cigarette. Theo did all these things plus tried to avoid ever leaving the house at all. She would sit in her room, hungry and light-headed, because she was too afraid to make the pilgrimage to the taco lady's truck if the boys were on the corner. And they were almost always on the corner. Sometimes Theo tried to go to sleep early, a trick she'd learned from reading depression-era books about poor parents trying to distract the kids from their hunger. But the few times Theo tried going to sleep hungry she just tossed and turned, holding her forehead where a terrible hunger headache lived.

The taco lady had to put up with the boys' antics sometimes.

"Oh, you want me to pay? I thought it was free," Theo'd heard the boys say to her.

The taco lady would stand stoically, wordlessly in front of them until they fell into a quiet respect and paid.

Around noon, if Theo wasn't at work she'd change the channel from Taco Lady TV to Thug TV and start watching the boys on the corner shout at girls or fuck with each other or smoke a blunt, and late night when she was sleeping she'd be awoken by Screeching Tire TV where some of those same boys would get into their classic cars and start doing donuts in the intersection until their cars were obscured by the smoke of tires burning on pavement. The first time Theo had raised her blinds in the middle of the night and seen the smoke she'd panicked, wondering if there was actually a fire.

Despite her hatred for being woken in the middle of the night by the boys with their bullshit donuts, Theo had always wanted a classic car. She wanted a 1965 baby blue Chevy Nova with its simple lines, like the drawing of a car in a coloring book.

What would her neighborhood in New York look like? She lit what she hoped would be the last cigarette of her life and paced the perimeter of the roof taking in the dome of City Hall and a few faint stars hovering shyly above the lights outlining the Bay Bridge.

She tried to make herself feel some emotion about leaving a city she'd lived in for ten years but she felt only felt hungover and cold. Theo often went through life comparing her void of emotion to characters in movies. If she were a character in a movie she'd get teary looking at City Hall, or have an epiphany about moving all the way across the country. At the very least she'd feel the devastating, crushing blow of knowing she would never watch a *Forensic Files* episode again on the tiny black and white TV.

She'd gone out of her way in life to feel nothing and now maybe it had backfired the same way getting drunk every day and learning nothing in high school had backfired. She was almost thirty and had no idea what made a moon full or what countries bordered which in the world. Once she'd bought a shower curtain with a map of the world to make up for the high school geography classes she'd been too drunk to learn anything in. But after bragging to everyone about Italy being the boot, she'd turned the other way in the shower, irritated at her absence of knowledge.

Her lip throbbed. She'd forgotten about her bar injury from the night before.

"I'm not drinking in New York," she'd said, trying to get as drunk as possible to compensate for all the drunks she'd never have again.

Her friends had thrown her a going away party, a last hurrah, and she'd accidentally bitten through her lip when a friend had flung her straight off the dance floor into a cement pillar. She felt ashamed. She was too old to be having "bar injuries." She took a drag from her cigarette and hung her head over the edge of the roof-top. A green city garbage truck idled and Theo saw the remnants of a giant supermarket sheet cake lying next to some dirty diapers. A breeze swept the fumes from the garbage truck right into her face. She felt her stomach turn and then she retched a liquid pile of mostly gin and tonics littered with tiny pieces of undigested orange cheese.

"See you later San Francisco," she said as she stood up.

If life could be started over any time any place why not start over in New York where a person could find out if they're an artist or at the very least purchase a slice of pizza any hour of the day? Theo's belongings were already loaded in her truck. By the time she got to New York her hangover would be gone, her head would be clear and she would be something! An artist! An entrepreneur! An inventor! She had so many ideas: the toilet cup — with its tagline, "Don't drink out of the toilet! Drink out of the toilet cup!" It would be a travel mug in the shape of a toilet with a toilet seat that went down for a lid. She'd also always wanted to make a mood ring for alcoholics — the catch, whatever color the stone changed would still translate into the word, "sorry."

She heard laugher and when she looked around she saw the terrible boys from the corner standing on the roof of the projects across the street. Her impulse was to duck down and hide but she remembered she was moving to New York as soon as she finished what was now the fifth of her last cigarettes ever, and so she felt less afraid. She watched their silhouettes move and tried to listen to their indistinguishable murmurs. Their laughter sounded drug induced. Theo watched as they walked together to the edge of the roof. She was scared they were looking at her and she stood very still. What if they tried to do something crazy like slingshot a stone into her face? A few weeks ago they had a slingshot and were using pigeons as target practice.

"Now," she heard one of the boys say and all four heaved a long duffel bag over the side of the roof. The bag fell fast and heavy, hitting the top of taco lady's makeshift awning with a large *thwap*! Then the awning slowly gave way, its aluminum poles splaying slowly out like a tired giraffe's legs. Theo looked over the side of her roof and saw the taco lady bending over the duffel bag that was lying on top of the collapsed blue tarp. The taco lady screamed twice and Theo heard the sharp yelp of a dog.

Real Paper Letter

Tamara Llosa-Sandor

"Dispiriting things – . . . A letter from the provinces
that arrives without any accompanying gift. You might
say the same for a letter sent from inside the capital,
but this would contain plenty of things you wanted to
hear about and interesting news, which makes it a very
fine thing to receive in fact . . ."

— Sei Shonagon, *The Pillow Book*

Living in Eugene is like dating a girl you're slightly embarrassed by. Why are you dating her? You're not entirely sure. It's the kind of thing that makes you blather nonsense, the hysteria mounting as you fumble for justification. Maybe the right words just don't exist. Not as in it's so wondrous there are no words in all of history to express what expansion your heart feels; it's more that you're stumped. You don't know why you two are dating. How did you end up here? How did you end up with her? But, she has some good traits, you say, attempting to elaborate. Though, always, as soon as you begin, there seems immediately to arrive a contradictory sign that just overwhelms your attempt, like the young vaguely hippie methhead at the bar wearing a neon pink vest with scrawled sharpie on the back that reads, "I EAT PUSSY."

Here she is. Meet Eugene.

❦

I arrived on the overnight train around noon on a Tuesday. It seemed a romantic, old timey, not to mention cheaper way of leaving one place and pulling into another. Because Amtrak is like a time portal I could forget, or try to forget, what it was in fact I was leaving. Could I rewind time, forge into an alternate reality, as if I had made a different choice all along? Or perhaps I could simply hit pause by leaving a place where everything is in a constant state of renewal for a place where everything is suspended in different phases of past expiration. Could one really disappear into a different era? Arriving in Eugene was like arriving eight years ago: not enough time passed to gather a vintage aura, but rather the cultural delay fifth or sixth cities bore in their geography. It was eight years ago, fifteen, thirty, but always with that lag; perhaps it was a stall-out within a slow-motion collision of particularly freaky moments in our country's history — hippie, crusty nouveau environmentalist bike gearhead hippie, raver, raver tweaker, grunge raver tweaker white Rasta deadhead, lesbian separatist, separatist academic trickster coyote ancestral storyweaver sociologist ensnared in the yarns of three-decade-old jargon. More on that later. Either way, my old life was further away for having traveled by train. I remembered it only as something odd, like dreamlife. Did all that really happen? The old life receded, overshadowed by the terminal present.

❦

I was willing to tell the prospective roommates, my interviewers, anything they wanted to hear. I never cook meat. I'm as green as a leprechaun. Absolutely the environment is a priority. Sustainability? It's my motto. I've been composting for years. Cooking communal meals is my greatest joy. Oh yes every weekend I go to the Farmer's Market just to talk to the farmers. Music? Strictly singersongwriters . . . or bluegrass . . . or, wait, what do you like? Oh, yeah, me too. No, I never watch TV. Unless you guys watch TV. You don't? Okay, then never. Your pets are so sweet! What are their names? What are a few fleas! Of course I don't write passive aggressive notes.

The last one was true, though later I realized we had varying opinions on the difference between passive aggressive and just plain aggressive.

❦

I am reborn into suburban grocery shopping — empty parking lots, wide aisles, bulk stacks, jars and cans, jars and cans.

❦

Let the days of oversized flannels and the nights of blanket jackets begin.

❦

Eugene Weekly, Letters to the Editor: "How can we afford prevention laws and police forces for Deadheads dancing under the influence of mushroom intoxication, and not afford to educate our children?"

❦

Deep in the clutches of sincerity.

❦

Even with its multi swirling plaids and greasy neon hairstyles of the 1990s, I wondered if irony had ever penetrated the perimeter of town.

❦

When you're biking and some driver is cutting the car too close, or not letting you into the lane for a left turn, it isn't worth flipping them off because the driver will then pull alongside you for a PEACE SUMMIT.

"Hey! Why'd you flip me off? Why are you spreading hate?"

Since he seems to be pacing me for multiple blocks, I ask, "Do you want to take me for a cup of coffee to talk about it?"

"Noooooo-oh! I just don't know why you have to use a symbol of aggression. Why don't you consider love? You should really consider love!"

Finally we get to a stop sign, and I've gathered my thoughts. "Hey man, I'm on my way to yoga. Don't even talk to *me* about love!"

❦

What's it called when optimism is so relentless it verges on nihilism?

❦

I've noticed a lot of people on first dates at the one upscale café in town. Mostly undergrads. Mostly undergrads courting each other with unvaryingly high tales of visits to Amsterdam.

❦

I hope I don't stay here long enough to start dating undergrads.

❦

Will I stay here long enough to start dating undergrads?

❣

Eugene Weekly, Living Out, an article on seeing Joan Rivers' standup act: ". . . The lights dimmed and the audience cheered, including our back-row gang of four — four Jews, three chubby AARP card-carrying dykes, two breast cancer survivors, one wheelchair user. Bring on the comedy! . . . "

❣

I felt guilty laughing.

❣

Okay, I didn't feel guilty.

❣

Kinds of local guilt: white-guilt; privilege-guilt; white-privilege-guilt; education-guilt; middle-class-guilt; using-plastic-guilt; using-any-kind-of-chemical-guilt; owning-a-car-guilt; owning-a-television-guilt; not-composting-guilt; not-biking-more-guilt; long-showers-guilt; electric-dryer-instead-of-gas-dryer-guilt; asking-anything-of-restaurant-or-bar-waitstaff-guilt; having-an-able-body-guilt; making-a-snap-judgment-guilt; not-having-anything-nice-to-say-guilt; being-an-American-guilt; not-having-working-class-or-immigrant-narratives-in-your-recent-ancestral-past-guilt; belonging-in-general-to-the-first-world-guilt.

❣

I've started to go on what I can only call "practice dates." I only want to get involved with people I have no romantic interest in. That and people who are so far outside any previous friend circle that we are pretty much anonymous to each other. Not like prostitute anonymous, just so unknown that when I inevitably make a series of casual sex/drunk small talk gaffes, I one, won't go into the usual shame spiral, and two, don't have to worry about being the date's bad hookup story. It would be nice not to be featured in any more tales of obsessional love or tragic make-outs. Or, at least, let it be in some far, far-away sphere of gossip.

❣

But wait, back to the first precept: dating people of no romantic interest. Coming off twelve years worth of sequential monogamy, I was curious about the notion of "casual." What was it exactly? How did people keep from catching a bullet train straight to the land of commitment? If I liked someone, I was already onboard. How could I not be? But say if it was someone I didn't like? Was that the secret?

❣

I could sense a whole upcoming period of greatly reduced responsibility: a reduction towards my fellow humans, towards the "local community," perhaps even towards the grander notion of society itself. Being selfish seemed a matter of not letting much else interest you. Spirited as I usually was on the winds of others' enthusiasms, how unthinkingly attracted I was to shiny objects, that was going to be difficult. But I wanted to try. A new town could still be a new self, especially if I let the Facebook account go dormant. Could I be someone other than who I had been?

❣

When you were born a dork and knew you were a dork and later knew you weren't one of those cool dorks who would celebrate her lifelong dorkiness, but were the kind of dork who'd do anything to remove that taint from the historical record, and executed what you considered strategic choices at each social juncture, putting more and more buffer between you and that initial dork-self, only to then find yourself at thirty in intimate circumstance with the alternate adult person you could have all too easily become, the encounter will conjure such levels of unease it borders on pathological.

❧

Was the woman who asked me out that someone? Or, one of those someones? Was I looking into a future version of who I would've been had I the ability to go back in time and strike a different course? I was scared, and drew closer. She wore a fitted necklace with a Chinese character imprinted on oval tab, choker-like, right at her collarbone; loose light blue jeans, grey running sneakers, a zip-up fleece, and a beanie that matched her skin tone and made her head look like one unblemished pink egg.

I guess I'd categorize her as an older sporty butch, though she seemed to lack the bravura of sporty butches I'd formerly brushed against. She did have a cockiness, but it was more of the melancholy variety, a long-suffering heaviness that hung about. She hunched, both heavily, wearily, and also from the muscles she had gathered rock climbing. Everything was a potential metaphor of stoical feeling and great sadness. She too remembered when she was still reeling from a breakup. She too was alone on the rockface of an unfamiliar city. She too had felt the depths.

❧

The drink date was a rapid metering of questions. I guess she was feeling me out to see how single I was, see how long I'd been out of a relationship, see if I was, I don't know, companionable?

I did my best to repeat her questions back to her. It was mutual tabulation.

Was it sorrow that I'd initially detected? Or . . . I thought I heard the ancient sound of dial-up modem in the distance . . .

The computer-y-ness made sense as she'd worked in the InterWeb world and had only recently left. Now she was enrolled in a graduate program for journalism and communications. Dissertation subject: on-line gaming culture. Specifically: expressions of masculinity.

❣

So, what you're saying is when men get together anonymously on the Web in a competitive atmosphere, they end up saying shitty things about women, homosexuals, and racial minorities?

❣

After the drinks were all ice, she asked if I wanted to go out again. She was watching me unlock my bike. Like a date-date, I said. Yeah, she said, a date-date. I didn't say anything while I reattached the troublesome bike lights. She cut into the silence, Well, why don't you think about it and call me. I looked at her. Time to test the new self. I said, I don't have to think about it but what you need to know is I'm only interested in having drinks then having sex, I don't want anything to do with responsibility right now, so if you can handle that we can have a date.

Holy shit. I couldn't believe it! I'd never said anything like it before! Was this the freedom you gained when you chucked romance altogether?! But — was I really going to have sex with this person? Would I in fact beg this future alternate version of myself to have sex, with painfully forward language about her rock climber arms? Was this who I was, who I could've been? Freedom, who the hell were you? Somewhere, in that distant dial-up sound, I heard the ring back, eerie, a breakdown, oncoming, ping ping . . . ping.

❣

As it was a college-hippie town with a dark meth underbelly and exceptional social services compared with the rest of the region, everywhere in Eugene harbored the homeless, the vagabond youth, the junkies, the weathered alcoholics, the men with Harley bandanas and hook hands, but there was a particular wedge of town that had a magnetic lure for the all-sorts. The scene, so to speak, was a very fertile botanic garden of Eugene flora, springing from what I'm going to call Needle Park. The park was behind a BBQ joint, across the street from a rowdy, itty-bitty tavern, catty corner to a parking lot shared by an organic grocery and a divorced-dad-apartment-complex. It was a stone's-throw from an AA meet-up and just round the way from a Japanese izakaya. It was just steps from the courtyard of a bakery/café that served the local specialty, a brown rice and black bean bowl, as well as gluten-free pastries, all of which was pleasant enough though you'd be eating in the court-yard on the off-chance it wasn't raining and the tweaker who was becoming a little too familiar with you would circulate at least three times asking for spare dollars. The patron's responses were varied, from the not-an-addict-guilt of handing over of a dollar, to the "not while I'm eating" brusqueness, to the simple "Sorry," to which most of the junkies did some form of beatific bow and said, "Sorry? What for?" before forgetting the whole exchange and hustling through the courtyard again fifteen minutes later.

Anyway, the anchor of this particular neighborhood nexus was the local honky-tonk. Tuesdays for bluegrass, Mondays for Bingo, always for music at seven, always for cheap cocktails, overly hoppy microbrews, and two-dollar slices of day-old pizza.

❣

In the honky-tonk for the first time, the lez morosely swirled her jar of dark beer. She was explaining the meaning of heteronormativity. I was onto a third whiskey soda, things getting a little swimmy in my periphery. There were the usual Eugene characters and the many tables were filling up. Several of the regular, weathered old guys were swinging by tables of people they knew. There seemed a whole orchestration of them, or maybe just enough for a jam band. The lez paused from her beer swirling to take in the scene. She sipped the porter and shook her crown of heavy thoughts. She swirled the beer and pulled in her lips. She shook her head decisively now. She sighed, "Expressions of Masculinity."

❣

We made out in the front of her pickup, idling at the rose garden outside my apartment. I could hear the expressions of masculinity on a nearby park bench enforcing positivity on each other. Who Told You You Couldn't Sing? Carrying A Tune Is All In Your Mind, Man!

❣

Later I stood on the mini step that functioned as a porch to my apartment. I smoked a cigarette in the damp and cold, and listened to the guys on the park bench. I thought about companionship. I thought about loneliness. I huddled into my many mismatched layers and thought about guys in the honky-tonk and their many mismatched layers. What would happen if I stuck around long enough?

Sister Spit 2010 Tour Diary

Nicole J. Georges

As we pulled out of New York, we passed a movie set where two people practiced tossing a cat back & forth. Our Cats on Broadway* destiny realized!

We played at an outdoor venue on Bard's vast campus. Every couple disappeared at some point separately, only to return covered in grass + claiming to have been "Star gazing."

The advice girl told us she had a copy of "Go Ask Alice" at her house.

As we waited for our friends to return from inside her house, we feared the worst.

*IN MONTANA WE PASSED A Vet called "Cats On Broadway," & had a running joke about felines in tophats & canes ever since.

Who Knows the Secret to the Pleasure of a Woman?

Tara Jepsen

Lights come up. I am seated at a table with two gay male writer friends. A beautiful singer stands to the side of us and starts playing the theme song to this section, "Who Knows the Secret to the Pleasure of a Woman?" The song finishes with its eponymous phrase.

All seated writers (in answer to "Who knows the secret. . . ?"): WE DO.

Marcus: Tara, are you willing to enlighten us slovenly manfolk as to your erotic leanings?
Tara: I am.

(to audience)

In my lesbian fantasy I'm shoved out of a car driving on the highway at moderate speed. I'm wearing a knee-length skirt, a simple cotton shirt with a collar, and I tumble out like a mess of broken broomsticks across the gravel and into the grass. It is dusk. I land next to a frog whose bagpipe body expands and contracts with a necessary function. I lie on the warm earth and listen to the frog's vocal rubber band boinging. I think of Foley artists. I think I am, for the moment, fully alive.

In my lesbian fantasy I live in a home entirely "furnished" with the most beautiful fake bear rugs with fake bear heads. White walls with dark wood trim surround me. The back door opens to a humming snarl of green. I eat fruit and drink wine and have one bear rug designated for sleeping and my back never hurts. The other rugs are for entertaining guests and we're always lying down but also sitting up. A fire crackles to the degree that we need it. It is always the mood of being liquefied butter. There is a notion of bongs but no reality of them. If I ever have to move to a new home I just roll up the rugs, break all the wine glasses in a detached and joyful ceremony, and pack up my big Chevrolet van. I have help though I don't need it. Setting up a new home is simple and the plumbing works perfectly including incredible water pressure. My hair is always frizzy and huge.

My pants never creep into my vagina. I remain limber though ambivalent about yoga. My friends also drive vans. I hang out with independent adults and a couple really cool thirteen-year-old boys. I care desperately for the environment and the only reason I don't sail around the world is I don't want to steer a ship all day. But I want to get lost in a wild pack of dolphins always. Not in a sexual way but also in a sexual way.

In my lesbian fantasy there are straight men sitting next to me explaining to each other how oppressed they are by their dates, they diagnose the women like idiots, throwing around terms like "schizophrenic." In my lesbian fantasy I stand up, ask them to move their chairs back, then I flip their table. I put one man on each of my shoulders and carry them out of the café into daylight and as we walk out I say, "See, now it's literal."

In my lesbian fantasy my fag friend Marcus Ewert and I have a detached and impassioned marriage. We love but are not IN LOVE. We need but we don't crave each other. Our lovemaking involves Marcus as some sort of warthog man-trunk in great command of his animalistic physical drives and emotionally developed tenderness. We are responsive to each other and our detachment allows impossibly long gazes into each other's eyes. We decided together that the only appropriate response to a society that does not value women is to make my needs and experience our priority. This works because I am hopelessly devoted to him and I make a tremendous bowl of popcorn. I am a broad-shouldered hippie sophisticate who communicates openly with Marcus and I cook healthy meals for us in a vast kitchen in Laurel Canyon. My turtle wanders as she pleases.

(addressing Marcus and Danny)

Tara: Gentlemen. Do you feel you know the secret to the pleasure of a woman?

Marcus: I do.

Danny: I do.

Tara: Then let us begin.

Training for Goddesses

Kat Marie Yoas

Many of these women already have their names picked out and a good handle on the business end of a whip. So you gotta wonder why they are in the Pro-Domme training course? I'd like to think they aren't confident in their techniques, but I'm beginning to wonder if they're here to show me up. I thought I understood my experience level as "beginner," but each passing moment I wonder if there's a lower level to start from. Perhaps pre-beginner, a shallow end where I can watch all the other mistresses and dominatrix dunk their slaves into the murky, deep-end depths. Using only their eyes. And maybe a well positioned eyebrow.

I want that power. I think.

Mistress Zada sat all of us potential dominatrices in a circle, the "priestess circle." *I want to invite all of you powerful women to work here as Priestesses and Goddesses at Holy Mountain.* Holy Mountain isn't into words like "lady of the evening" or "pro" or even "domme," we aren't regular sex workers here we're priestesses. I like that, when I walk through the doors I'm not some broke lady burning some dude's precious feet for eighty bucks. They don't even allow cigarettes in this place. No, here I'm a priestess exacting some goddess-y revenge.

In that same line of thinking, Holy Mountain doesn't really look like a dungeon, at least any that I've seen in Disney Movies. There's no stone walls or shackles in plain sight. It really just looks like a fancy loft — a place that I actually feel more uncomfortable in than I probably would in a dungeon. However, there are some things here that aren't in your run-of-the-mill city loft apartment space. There are cages and ropes and a huge toilet, for a human toilet. Everything is hidden and what isn't is very tasteful, all gray and lavender — very soothing and expensive.

I'm not really the fancy-loft kind, or the professional dominatrix type, if there is one, but I needed the money and I like a challenge. I had the great idea to become a professional dominatrix after my girlfriend said I would be the worst dominatrix ever. It was a dare, her slumped at a bar stool: *You'd be the worst,* she laughed into her beer. *But, you know, we do really need the money, if you don't mind embarrassing yourself. Maybe you should just hook instead.* Jeff was a fellow who liked his feet burned with cigarettes by a small gang of giggly ladies. Believe me; it's easy to giggle in such situations. He lay there with a pair of socks in his mouth and I almost peed my pants. *I really held that situation together, man. I can't help it, you either have it or you don't.* I went to the bathroom of the bar and did some positive affirmations. I mean, sure, in a perfect world, I would have preferred that she encourage me, that she wouldn't hang out at this druggie bar, but this is what it is. A dare through insults, trial by fire. Whatever. Nobody is perfect.

It is a business. I mean, the whole domme thing. I can see through the priestess hoo-ha. We are in-call professionals at this lofty dungeon and after we give Mistress Zada a cut of our earnings, we make about two hundred bucks a session. So, lack of natural ability aside, this is the job for me. Clearly. I'm so broke I have to steal toilet paper — in fact I stole some from the dungeon about ten minutes before training began — but basking in the lavender priestess light I realize those days are behind me.

Mistress Zada had quiet power; she was the crystal-wearing type. The other girls looked like suicide girls or goth sluts, whichever term you prefer. I myself was wearing overalls and several pairs of socks. I felt overdressed. *Ladies, I'd like you all to only use your priestess names, from here on out.*

I truly don't know anything about practicality and this was a case in point. I hadn't thought this far into it. In preparation I didn't get any outfits nor did I think about a professional name. Instead, I practiced. I yelled at my refrigerator, humiliated my pillow and teased the sofa. I stomped on the floor and tried on being, you know, sexy and mean. I was attempting to achieve the magical balance between psychotic Mommie Dearest and the boyish cruelty of a young Matt Dillon. I had to stop after cajoling the oven. It was no use — I'd have to get trained. However, I wasn't anticipating a naming situation. Evidently, the other mistresses were.

Mistress Magdalene, Lady Isobel, Mistress Mara, all these mistresses ready to go.

Just pick a name based on your inspiration, your character, your priestess calling. I had to go with the flow, just pick a name, like it was so simple. I closed my eyes and envisioned my true nature. I was Rusty James in *Rumble Fish*, wanting to be in this gang but only possessing the desire, the guts, and not the brains or knowhow. And so I was born Mistress Rusty James. They looked adequately disgusted with my name and shortened it for me to Mistress James.

I wasn't the only clueless priestess; soon all sorts of confusion erupted around the circle.

How many slaves expect us to eat shit?

Mistress Magdalene, upon her wealth of shit eating questions, was revealed as clueless as to the whole point of being a dominatrix.

I was thrilled. I had a shit eating grin on my face, to honor both the clueless Mistress Magdalene and the dumbstruck Mistress Zada.

Mistress Zada was patient at first.

No, Mistress Magdalene, you never have to eat shit, you never have to do anything you don't want to, this is about pleasing yourself. They do what you want them to.

Mistress Magdalene rephrased: I just wanted to know what happens if they tell me to "eat brown."

Mistress Zada's eyebrows narrowed, then raised dramatically, then narrowed again, conveying their own secret messages to the shit eaters in the room. It was around this time Mistress Magdalene broke open a bottle of wine she had stashed in her spare boots. I was looking better every minute; the gloating was doing wonderful things for my complexion.

Because I'm not gonna eat shit. I don't think so, anyway — well, how much would that pay, cos if I had to, you know, go brown, I'd want to be reimbursed, you know for that right, that act.

Priestesses don't have to do anything they don't want to do. In fact, if in a session, you aren't sure where you see the session going or perhaps need a moment to regroup, you may put your slave in his starting position and take priestess time for yourself.

Mistress Zada said "priestess time" the same spa commercial way she said everything else. She was this dominatrix guru-type; she wasn't flogging a slave, she was getting her inner goddess pampered. I needed her brain in my brain. Pronto.

Mistress Magdalene was drunk already. The wine disappeared as magically as it appeared in the first place. I was processing the notion of time-outs during sessions; doing the math on how many I could possibly take without the slave feeling ripped off when the slaves arrived.

The slaves came in complete naked. I felt even more

overdressed. They all called themselves Jeff. It wasn't any fair, this fake name business. Their fake names were boring and bound to confuse me. I was having a hard enough time answering to Mistress (Rusty) James. All the slaves were alike, all white, the same height, the same mushroom cap penises. It had been a good five years since I saw a penis in real life. I didn't remember them looking like little doorknobs, round cartoon character noses sitting where their privates should be.

We were to pair off, to do energy sharing and trust exercises. I chose the mysterious and sexy Lady Isobel but was informed that I couldn't choose another priestess. This was America, I was a goddamn dominatrix, a goddess, I should be able to choose whoever I wanted, but no, I wouldn't even get to choose a mushroom cap slave. They were to choose us. Typical.

It was like a prison lineup. Let's just say if it was, I would have been a free man, an innocent. That wasn't the case, of course. All it meant was that no one chose me. It was too much, I needed Priestess Time already. I fled into the bathroom, harnessing my inner goddess, sashaying and nodding while I felt a strong need to whimper. Someone knocked at the door and I barked, *Priestess Time!* I stared into the mirror, any of these Jeffs would be so lucky for me to even look at them. I scowled at myself in the mirror then I smiled then I winked and channeled the genius of L'Oreal marketing and whispered "because you're worth it!" to myself. After the pep talk, I slipped some Q-tips in my pocket to take the edge off.

The energy and trust exercises were just like I remembered all trust exercises from my youth, totally terrifying and ridiculous. I hear "trust exercise" and think of those trust falls. I pictured a naked slave standing with his back to me, my legs bent slightly in the strong and ready position, his whimpers reaching my ears "Mistress James please don't let me fall!" And then, I do, of course, let him fall because he doubted me in the first place. I will be a cruel, middle school bully of a mistress. They will love me for it. But there were no trust falls. I got paired off with some Jeff and we sat facing each other in folding chairs. We were to maintain eye contact while I pinched and played with his nipples.

I should say I've never done a trust fall; instead, I would close my eyes and pretend to relax and fall. I just couldn't let go. I would stiffen and catch myself, every time.

I stared into this Jeff's eyes. They were dark pools of something intimate and open. I reached my very deliberate hands toward his chest. I raised an eyebrow. I went in for the kill. I missed. I missed Jeff's nipples. I missed them by a lot. But, as a Priestess, a Pro, I didn't look away. I maintained eye contact. I studied his look of surprise and unexpected pain as I rifled around his chest blindly. Like a raccoon in a trash can. I channeled the raccoon. I became Mistress Rusty James, raccoon priestess. I made my way to his nipples and I was gone. Every gasp or little sigh of pleasure from the Jeff's mouth left me groundless. I was in a blind trust fall. Every gasp and I was falling backwards into some place where there was no one behind me, no reaching arms. I was falling and just falling forever, with each pinch and twist and sigh I was letting go in the darkness, away from the mistresses and the Jeffs and towards nothing — no hands, no one to catch me. And just like that, Mistress Zada called time.

I should have had some of Mistress Magdalene's wine, that was for certain. She looked to be having a grand time; she had a wine moustache and continued pinching her Jeff's nipples looking off into space well after Mistress Zada told us to stop.

The Jeffs then got to assess our efforts. Mistress Magdalene was terrifying and should have kept eye contact. Lady Isobel was deep and sensual. I was playful and childlike. I wanted to barf. It seemed unfair. I didn't think they should be allowed to think or evaluate us. My Jeff also said he would like to work with me again. I was sort of flattered, but mostly was just calculating the distance between more money and increased priestess time.

Mistress Zada took me aside to tell me that both Lady Isobel and I showed promise. She asked if I'd like to administer Cabt. Cabt, I was rapt, it sounded pretty good, not so eye-contact driven. Sure, I said, completely clueless and probably a little high and stupid from the trust exercises.

Cabt was an acronym, turns out. It's C.A.B.T as in, cock and ball torture. The men stood in the lavender inner sanctum of the dungeon and I watched as Mistress Zada demonstrated and tied shoelaces around their mushroom dicks and sent them spinning like tops or New Years Eve party favors. Priestess Time, take two.

I was having a Sally Field situation. There were tears and laughter. I paced and stared at the human toilet set up in the shower. Was that always there? I started murmuring to myself the word penises. Penises whispered mid sob, laugh, through gritted teeth. I don't have a problem with penises, truly, but there were too many to look at and it had been so long since I had seen even a solitary penis. And that was a penis I had a crush on, a penis I loved.

Priestess time! I heard the knock before it even occurred. I was that in tune with the world around me. I dried off my face, tried to look like a person who had just applied lipstick or took a satisfying trip to the bathroom and left to return to the dungeon.

Mistress Zada was holding a machine. It was square-ish. I'm not good with electronics, but it looked like one.

Mistress Rusty James, we were waiting for you. I thought you'd enjoy this.

Jeff lay flat on the table next to the machine, flanked by priestesses. I tried to look competent and knowledgeable about the electronic square box. Mistress Zada handed me some rubber band bracelets and EKG looking devices.

Now, just put these on the base of his penis, and you can put the sticky parts on his testicles!

Sure!!!

Mistress Zada was cruel, man; this was her line of work. Give the job to the lesbo. I kept nodding enthusiastically and tried to have surgeon hands.

Make sure not to pinch! We only want the good pain here.

Putting a bracelet around testicles is not as easy as it sounds. Pulling the bracelet taut is also difficult. My hands were sweaty, his business was sweaty and I kept pulling my hands away as if darting from a feisty tiger. There was some yelling on his part and a lot of empathetic cooing from the Priestesses on the behalf of our pinched Jeff. Finally, he was completely accessorized.

Now, have you done work with electricity before?

Basically, he was hooked up to an electrocution device. I could program it to be light or hard, vary the rhythms and degrees of pain. It could even be hooked up to an Ipod or a microphone. Everyone played with the rhythms. I was starting to itch for more Priestess time when Mistress Zada handed me the microphone.

Here, have a go.

I stood next to Jeff's electrified penis and testicles; I lowered myself onto a chair so I was eye level with the spectacle. I opened my mouth and closed it, what do I say to a slave's penis? I was tongue-tied. What would a mistress say? I closed my eyes and the words came.

Hey hey mama say the way you move, gonna make you sweat, gonna make you groove . . .

Led Zepplin's "Black Dog" poured from me, I sang my heart

out. Jeff writhed around on the table, I knew all the words and Mistress Zada and the other priestesses were silent.

Didn't take too long before I found out what people mean by down and out . . .

After my performance, we were done with the day's trainings. I don't know how it happened, but everyone said they would work with me again.

I took one last priestess time in the bathroom. I was exhausted. I could feel my creation rising and falling inside my chest, a sighing Rusty James, my heart going so fast. I wanted to wait until everyone else left the dungeon. When I came out, the lights were dim. Everyone was gone. The windows of the loft were frosted with winter. Outside, I could see the Mistresses in their coats, the dressed slaves huddled together on the corner. I could feel the harshness outside, broke ass people living together in Chicago in the winter. All the slaves and the goddesses together, sharing a smoke.

I left the loft and took the long way home, me and Rusty James walking with the wind. I knew I'd never be back. I had other things to do. If I could manage to somehow trick those slaves into thinking I was in control, that I was powerful, imagine what I could do for my own self. I was as broke as ever, but this time, I felt broke in half, flung wide open to something.

I wanted to walk forever. I wanted to go home. I wanted my mom.

I took the train back to my girlfriend instead. Before I opened the door I thought, if she's home, I'll stay. If she's at the bar, I'm taking my priestess self right out of here. I felt electric and I put my keys in the door wiggled the doorknob and pushed.

Pandora

Sara Seinberg

There was no weather then. It was the time before we even had
a word for weather. There was just the day and the night, and a
stray thunderbolt when Zeus threw a tantrum. Seasonal cold fronts
and twisters and monsoons came later. This was before snow and
drought and turmoil. Under a perfect sky we'd read about Orpheus
in the bustling agora at the newsstand. He was just a small story
then, in a new zine these girls from Crete were putting out. While
most of the newsstand remained awash in the latest scandals of
Zeus and Hera, Persephone and I scoured the back of the stands
for journals and obscure quarterlies among the paper-wrapped
porn, vomitorium guides and fantastically popular *Orgy Advisor*.
The glossy covers of *Ambrosia This Week* and Zeus' self-promoting
Rolling Thunder served to vindicate my own godlessness. I wanted
nothing to do with the roving clots of girls costumed in their various
goddess-wannabe uniforms. The Athenas had their strong points, to
be sure; the home team in Athens with their very own temple to frequent. Ladies with their Aphrordite poses were a flush of aesthetic
bliss, but for me it was too much to strive for the impossible. And

my inherent state of otherness didn't allow for gang identification anyhow. Still so young at 128 years old, I had at least learned that.

But I suppose if it had to be someone it'd be Artemis. Her groupies had the best style, rippling arms and chests so muscular their breasts seemed to vanish. They went out in a pack to the forests at night like famished wolves, their shields at the ready, hauling quivers of hand-tooled arrows across their broad backs as if they weighed nothing. When the sun fell, the girls replaced their olive branch tiaras with hearty strips of leather cut from a group kill, tying back their ignored tresses. The boldest of the pack hacked off their own locks and roamed Greece in short hair that stood on end, a field of middle fingers toward Olympus, flipping Zeus off in his pursuit of any damsel, refusing to be the kind of woman any God would try to take down in a field of flowers.

It isn't just her worshippers either. Artemis is always good to me in her visitations. She is patient, teaches me useful things for my strange life: tanning hides for long journeys into the tundra, moving through any landscape in relative silence, hand to hand combat, and of course, archery. She is never distracted by affairs of emotional entanglement, has a pure focus on survival and duty. Nothing like her twin Apollo, yet she understands him implicitly. When they visit together they never speak, but rather intuit the other's language and come across as one voice.

Artemis never, NEVER, underestimates what a woman can accomplish. People say she's a virgin, the goddess of the virgin. Unlike the other lady Gods who come calling on me while I sleep, I figure she's too busy for men. And growing up in Zeus' Olympus, why not? It's always been difficult for me to understand what any woman sees in the humans who embody his example.

Persephone has her own following of girls, and like my best friend they wear their togas too low, darken the rims of their eyes with the ash of burnt cedar, and stalk pleasure the way the Artemis girls stalk prey. These girls make batches of lavender and sandalwood oils and dab the scent on pulse points where absolutely no one should be sniffing girls their age. They make their mothers nervous, provoking in the older women feelings of fear and pride, an anxiety cocktail. All mothers want their daughters to be beautiful, but not dangerous-beautiful. Certainly not in a city like Athens. These girls forget that Persephone has no age, that she will remain forever at the perfection of a ripened peach. And when you live forever, the notion of consequence is a continually receding concept.

Persephone's mother never treated her like a goddess, just like any other daughter. Any other bewitching, gorgeous, smoldering, perilous daughter. Demeter had, of course been around longer than her daughter, but in the Olympian culture, "longer" was so relative, it fell away within a few centuries. But while time sloughed off like dry skin, their mother/daughter thing never budged. Demeter kept tabs on Persephone like a mortal. She always wanted to know where her daughter was going, with whom, and when she'd be home. She critiqued her outfits as too risque, knowing all the while that it would never matter what the girl wore, everyone would want her, no matter what. Persephone had found her ways of getting around it all. Lying, stashing a whole wardrobe at Athena's temple for adventures, collecting lovers like chocolates across Greece. And what Persephone wanted that day, was Orpheus.

Blackened Deity had been playing roving forest shows for months and we had missed every one. Tale had been told of the enchanted singer, a voice so beautiful even the Sirens flew from their island to spy on him. The band was turning sound inside out, scraping lyre strings with jagged stones and setting up varying piles of hollowed drums for different sounds. It was said that an Artemis girl was the drummer, affixing a pedal to the biggest of the drums, and stomping on it in a half crouch while she beat on several others with different sticks. The zine reviewed the band's last show calling it "a secret forest delirium," "a moon-driven madness," "haunting hysteria." By the end of the review, so much alliteration had been employed I thought I might pull a muscle rolling my eyes. But Persephone was stuck on the sparse line drawing of the singer. She looked like a woman in search of dessert.

I arrived at her house with my basket of wool for spinning and my needles. The idea of sitting at the house staring at Demeter and making an afghan seemed just as delightful to me as sneaking out to find the band. Demeter spent her evenings sipping blush wine and relaxing by a fire. She always had a chill when the sun sank below the horizon. The wine and the fire kept her warm. Sometimes after a few glasses, when she lit up the wood, she would laugh about Prometheus sticking it to Zeus with the fire, but then she'd catch a glimpse of me there in the orange light, my jar always next to me, and she'd press her perfect lips together into a brick of silence.

She and Persephone didn't visit in my sleep the way the rest of the Gods did. I hung out with them all the time. They'd seen me at sixteen and they'd seen me at eighty-eight. They'd seen my first cigarette and my first broken hip. It seemed that in spite of my repeat visits to the ages, my brain mimicked the human experience of each number regardless of my years of experience. The first time I hit forty I was really only here for eight years, but the second time I was a hundred and four. I arrived naked in the shadow of the mountain at thirty two, then time marched with me up to eighty-eight, and — unlike my human companions — my body then recounted its edges as the sun continued to rise and set. My friends continued dying as my spine re-stacked itself regal and strong. Time marched me back to sixteen, and then I woke up one day and I just knew, I could just feel it rushing through me. I was on my way back to eighty-eight.

I don't think the Gods even knew how I would work. Zeus used to visit a lot in the beginning, but as his plan suggested, women were only useful for two things, sex and deceit, so my usefulness was ignored. Thanks to Hera, his visits simply ended and my fate lost its director. I became a mystery to all of us, shuttling back and forth from maiden to spinster. I used to wait for Hera to visit, lay on the roof of Athena's temple to be closer to the sky and beg her to come, to explain what had happened. When she did come, only a couple times, she was so sad all she did was weep. I'd heard about her flamboyant bitchiness in the magazines, the fantastic performances of vindictiveness and jealousy the Greeks had come to admire and fear. But the last time Hera came to me, so many years ago, her hair was lanky, and filthy robes clung to her wet body as she sat in her river, broadcasting herself from the Middle Place, in exile from her luxurious home. I could see Sisyphus in the background, rolling the stone up the hill while Hera rolled joints. She'd smoke each one so fast, staring at me the whole time like a painting. And the higher she got, the more she cried. She was barely a goddess at all, let alone the Queen of the mountain. She would only say **I'm sorry, Pandora. I'm so so sorry**. After a long visit of saying nothing, I got up and sat in the river with her. She smelled good. Everything about her was like legend says, except her fingernails. She bit them down to a bloodline. I took her hands into mine and rubbed the saltwater from her river into the nailbeds while a friendly partridge did our hair, licking the salty tears up off her perfect skin.

❦

I was born on the mountain, fully grown, naked in the dusk wind gorged with the scent of the sea. My first visit with the gods was so quick, a montage of fierce beauty. They sent me down the mountain knowing they would visit me later, and I staggered out into the world to track down my fate, the jar in a velvet sack bobbing from a golden rope clutched in my new hands. My first stroll I cannot do justice, for the first of anything cannot live in the ineptitude of language. I filled my new lungs with the sweet wind, sagebrush and cedar, honeysuckle, and spearmint. And then, a figure. A lamb. I puffed outward at it, but she did not move. She looked at me still and ready, her big eyes steady and thick. Then blink. Blink. A lamb saying Hello. I walked toward her, somehow slow in my fervor, restraining the speed of my steps. And then, my nose. Her aroma bigger and bigger and finally it rippled over me, an avalanche in the center of my face, telling me all it could about the creature world.

Information arrived in mountainous ways and my birth into knowledge with no actual experience spoiled me with wonder. I knew the charm of each splendid creature would haunt me: the birds with their regal flight, the amphibious magical changelings. I knew an otter and its mad frenzied frolic, yet I had not laid eyes upon the sea.

The weight of it felled me, my knees in a meadow facing the mountain. My heart's first break within moments of life, it laid me open, shutting down my windpipe. My first tears were two things at once — a physiological miracle of wetness, and a vision of shackles hanging from the side of the mountain rock, empty and useless, not even swaying in the mighty wind. Where Prometheus had kneeled in anguish, bound. I knew at once the story of how I came to be, and this god I would hunt in the name of Zeus, this thief of fire and protector of man.

Then my first visit from Hera, a flicker of a beautiful woman, cackling and drunk, sipping a chilled venom by the sea cliffs. She filed her fingernails into hard crimson tools. The sun refusing to burn her narrow shoulders, her beauty a fact, a flawless fact that had long ago ceased to provide her with any comfort or joy. The marble nail file hissed around the small curves of her fingers as she stewed, a bubbling spite as constant as her unmarred skin. Eternal suffering trapped in a shitty union with her brother. Her philandering husband of a brother.

How can these mortals
understand anything?
They divorce,
they leave,
they sign papers and
trade children.
They think they
know pain.
Hera
knows pain.
I designed it
in my own image.
These foolish figures
pot their pain
by hyacinths in the
spring garden and
they tend it and
they sing to it.

Oh, pain, look
how lovely you are.
How formative.

They walk by
the shrubs of

elation and
let them run
weedy and wormed.
The worms flock
to the rich soil
while the gardeners
pour rosewater
onto betrayal and
empty promises
as if the act of
sweetening them
will turn them into trees.

Hera laughed. She barely saw me, even though it was she who has come calling. She was a blind goddess, wracked with a wretched zeal for revenge. And she was so beautiful, so utterly powerful, I couldn't help but start my life wanting only to please her.

And then she was gone. The wind was cold and my jar started its clamor.

It's been like this since I can remember. Zeus's father ate his siblings, and that was long before me and my famous jar. It seems difficult to believe that all the world's evils could be crammed into my purse when a god ate his kids right out of the gate. But still I run around in fear — centuries of mourning, mutilation, genocide, and epidemics. Simple broken hearts and humiliation. Useless betrayals, gout, slavery, a bubonic blackness, and ovens in Europe. Witches burned, children sold, and sailors drowned. Machetes in Rwanda, the angel of death flying over bloodied doorways in Egypt, Hiroshima, Irish car bombs, casual rape culture, and heroin. These things roam free, a herd of misery throughout time, but still, I lug the jar around, afraid it could get worse.

Don't open the jar, Pandora, they say. **Something terrible will happen.**

But terrible things happen constantly. You say a word like war and it's just three little letters. So easy. You put your lips together in a pucker, push a little air out and roll an r at the end. Easy word. But inside it, the unimaginable. Unless you are there. Then you don't have to imagine it, you have to live through it. Over and over, the rest of your small, mortal life. Mortar and mortal are only one letter away from each other. And that's just the English irony. All the languages have their jokes.

But the jar was a part of my birth, and so like an organ, I carted it around despite logic. Zeus had sent me to seduce Prometheus, who knew I was a trick. Zeus quickly came up with Plan B — to have me couple and cripple the dimmer Titan, Prometheus's brother Epimetheus. But Prometheus dragged Epimetheus away so fast that even Plan B was just a pile of cinders before I was the age of a toddler. The whole thing was such an immediate failure, the Gods forgot about me most of the time. They moved on to other things and eventually, their careless matings with other mortals brought more women. I was no longer the special one. Yet something had me march on, looking for the Titan brothers. That is what I'm hardwired to do, the purpose of my entire being. That and, thanks to Hera, women.

The jar was my constant companion. Each night I would lay with it in my arms, feeling the contents bang into its walls throughout my dreams. I clutched it to me protecting it from theft in the cover of darkness. I sang to it, songs of love and loss, and sometimes the saddest songs would quiet the thing, a city of nightmares in a jar. After a time I would set it away from me, needing my own sleep for strength and travel. From across the room I watched it by burning candles, the commotion settling into a night rhythm of humming and thumping until the sun broke. By the candlelight I could sometimes see a glow in there. It took years to become acquainted with the residents of the jar, but the longer I knew them the better I could see the glow.

Meanwhile the world spun on. Mortals made all kinds of discoveries after the theft of the fire. They found electric avenues and bands of sound. They made communication strides with devices, they took to the sea and the air for travel. They began to control the very cycles of women, create more and more means of quick murder in hot places, moving from hands to rocks to daggers to arrows to cannons to revolvers to lasers. They mapped poverty and drugs to wipe out swathes of populations. Humans spent so much time and money figuring out new ways to kill each other, one wondered if they understood they would all die at some point anyhow.

Sometimes I stared at the jar, and I wondered what I was. A product of gods, not even an orphan with parents to mourn, was I a mortal? Adrift in the world with no peers, I would sometimes come upon a god who showed me kindness, protected me as a product of Olympus; just as often I came across immortal cruelty, Ares showing off his warlike skills that would leave bruises for sixteen years. Hera sending me so many gorgeous women, each one irresistible and irreparably damaged. Signs of aging would come and go, my appearance would climb to a certain wrinkle and then as though a children's riddle, the wrinkles would fade and my breasts would inch back up my chest. And all the while, I'd follow the Titans across the globe, not quite understanding why, and I would watch my jar.

Belle

Kirk Read

I want to tell you a story about the most illegal thing Ed and I have ever done. This was early in our relationship, like three years in. If you're in a relationship and you hang out through the gnarly patches, you are rewarded with stories.

So we were at a Billy Club gathering, which is sort of like a faerie gathering except that it's sober and while the faeries are working out their issues with nail polish and sequins, the Billies are working out their issues with flannel and workboots. But all of these people have issues. We were at a gathering at Saratoga Springs and Ed was across the room snuggling with some guy and I was getting a backrub from this guy in overalls. We'd had a nice conversation so far but at first I view everyone with suspicion and a little derision. Just to be honest about that.

So the next day he says he wants to discuss a business idea with Ed and me and that we should come to his land in Laytonville. So we did. We weren't sure if it was going to be buying into his land or housesitting or what. It turned out that he was a small time pot grower and wasn't going to be around for most of the summer, so he wanted us to go up on weekends and water the twenty-five plants. He would buy the starters and set up the garden and we would water. And for that we would get 10 percent of the harvest. Which felt fine to us, I mean, what did we know? We were excited to have forty acres of land around us and this beautiful little handmade house. He'd built the house with his lover, who died of AIDS. They hadn't really insulated the place — the walls were made of those wooden vegetable box tops. Super charming, but a decidedly rural affair. The view from the deck was breathtaking. On a clear day you could see the ocean.

I should say right now that I don't even like pot. It leads to dorm room philosophical conversations and people say *Dude* and *Right on* a lot. I find this distasteful. So I don't really like pot but I do like money.

Kevin had a cat. Her name was Bill. I don't know why her name was Bill. And I'm the last person to be the gender police, but this was a fluffy gray longhaired cat with oversized whiskers. She was not Bill. She lived some of the time under the house, using a piece of pink insulation as a hammock. The first time we came to the house, he had locked her inside. There was no food out. Presumably there was a gay couple who would come by and feed her. They were also pot growers and they belonged to the ZZ Top genre of gay men. Long beards, rural neuroses, darting eyes. All year, they would shit and piss into buckets, then create a mixture so that at Christmas, their grower friends would receive a bucket of Mendocino's finest fertilizer. In contrast, my mother gives out peanut brittle at Christmas. On a cookie sheet with a toy hammer. You get to keep the cookie sheet and hammer.

We didn't see Kevin all that often. I would leave huge bowls of food for the cat, whom we renamed Belle, as in Beltane. It was a much better fit. Kevin left us a note in all caps that the food had attracted ants. But I kept leaving her lots of food and multiple bowls of water. I had a nightmare about gay ZZ Top leaving her bowls of shit and piss.

And Ed is a tall man, so twice he bumped his head on the propane lamps hanging from the ceiling. He broke two of the little mesh mantles in the lanterns and we got another all caps note from Kevin accusing us of being bad guests. He left us information about a store in San Rafael where we could replace the parts. It was like $12.

The actual watering of the plants was not all that difficult. There was a spring that fed the tank and you had to turn on a pump at the bottom of the hill to get it to the upper tank, then gravity would feed it to the twenty-five plants. At one point rats chewed through the tubes going to the plants, so we had to replace those. But it was pretty fun scrambling up and down the hills and operating machinery.

When harvest time rolled around, we learned from Kevin that we were expected to trim with him. Two of us, one of him. I didn't like that math. I started thinking about how we were only getting 10 percent and the injustice of it made me crazy. Sitting around a trim table, with all that pot seeping into your hands, you get this dull, foggy high and all you can do is angry math. It was a resentful trim.

The last night of the trim, Kevin was setting up a propane heater to speed the curing process in the guesthouse. This house was beautiful. It had cost something like $30,000 to build and it was small, but the floor was made of exotic hardwood with lots of design detail. All over the room, there were strings holding plants and our trimmed buds. Next to the propane heater, I had used a metal bucket and two pieces of metal fencing to steady the propane tank. Kevin had angrily dismantled my addition, saying that I didn't know what I was doing and that he was an intellectual. In the seventies, many of his friends were Prairie Fire. I asked him Were you

Prairie Fire? And he said that in the language of social Marxism, he couldn't decide if I was bourgeois or an adventurist youth.

Ed and I made dinner each night of the trim. The final night, I came to really resent the way we were cooking and cleaning, so I left the dishes for him to do. There was a rainstorm outside and Kevin looked at the dishes in the sink and said "I don't want to deal with this right now but I don't want Bill to get into them." And with that he picked up the cat, opened the door, and tossed her outside into the rain. He went into the bathroom. I went to the kitchen sink and got an eight-inch chef's knife and held it out in front of me. Ed said what he says when I'm doing something questionable: *What's happening?*

And I walked down to the woodstove. I heard the shower start. I waited, running my fingers along the blade to make sure it was sharp enough.

Ed said *Honey, put the knife down.*

I let the cat back inside and went to the bedroom and closed the door. I got on my knees on the bed and I put my hands up in the air in a diamond shape and started breathing heavily. Ed walked in and said what he says when I'm doing something odd. *What's happening?*

And I said *I see fire!*

The next morning Ed got up to make coffee and found Kevin at the kitchen table, all the color drained out of his face. He said there had been a fire in the night. The propane tank had tipped over as it ran out and the heating element burned a foot-wide hole in the floor. I didn't tell him about my spell. I had just gotten home from my first week of California Witchcamp and I was pretty satisfied with myself. Because if you can't hurt, you can't heal.

When it was time to drive the pot to the city, I made Kevin carry all of it in his vehicle. My 1986 gold Chevy Cavalier had stripes painted all over it, as well as pink leopardskin upholstery I'd made from remnants I got at Wal Mart. I was not about to be this man's drug mule. He passed off numerous plastic tubs which previously held nutritional supplement powder. I sold that pot and made $8500. And I hated that man with every transaction, knowing that he would never be able to sell his 90 percent. Knowing that he still had most of last year's harvest under the bed in the guest room.

To this day I regret not taking Belle with us or calling the SPCA. Some nights I'd kneel on the edge of my bed, my hands in a diamond pointing north, chanting

This cat must be free
This cat must be free
This cat must be free
This cat must be free

I don't know if it worked or not.

he Hong Moon Lesbians of the Sacred Heart

I sort of thought it was normal to be a lesbian, because it seemed like we were all lesbians at our island Secondary School.

It could be because it was a Catholic Convent girls' school, which seems to have a pattern of producing lesbians. Or it could be because of Ling Ling, who was the coolest girl in our school, and as queer as the sisters were pious.

But her coolness wasn't so much a credit to her as it was a credit to being American, and so you could argue that some of us were lesbians indirectly because of the command of the American empire.

While I realize that I could face some opinions to the contrary, especially from members of the school staff, these are to the best of my recollection, my own true and factual memoirs of growing up as one of the many lesbians of the Hong Moon Convent of the Sacred Heart.

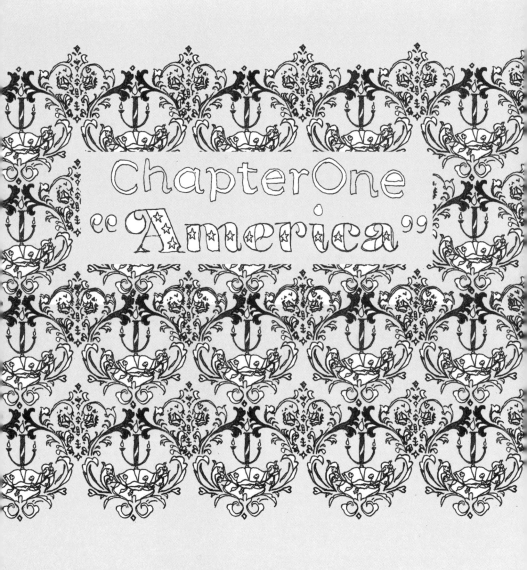

ChapterOne
"America"

There are 6 billion of us in the world who do not come from North America, and we know what it's like to live in its shadow - growing up hearing, seeing, reading, watching, discussing, interpreting and mildly obsessing over it.

But it's like sex. Until you really get to know it, your idea is inaccurate and exaggerated. As much as Americans have absurd exotic notions of every other country, we have absurd exotic notions about them. Except that instead of barely one single ignorant misconceived notion, we have infinite ignorant, misconceived notions.

And we have to entertain them all, because like sex, no matter what you think of it, you can't even try to escape it. You can't be disinterested or decide to ignore it. If you did, you would have to take up a radical alternative lifestyle like asexuality or religious service. It's indisputably powerful, and it pervades, influences and controls your life in an inevitable, insidious way. You might chase it, claim it, imitate it, condemn it or even fight it, but it won't go away.

"But wait," you might say. "I don't want to hear about America. I want to hear about the LESBIANS of HONG MOON."
Yes, that's true. But in order to explain the culture of my Hong Moon school and influential trendsetters like Ling Ling, I have to explain the idea of "America".

Especially in a capitalist consumer culture like Hong Moon, "America" is a welcome and influential actor. It determines local values, priorities, desires and peer pressure. And I don't mean America as in real-life everyday nine-to-five paying-the-rent America - but "America," the shiny inflated exported image of the Leader of the Free World.

To explain this exotic notion of "America," I've taken a Hong Moon survey.

facebook

Elisha Lim
What was your first impression of the U.S.A.?

17 hours ago · Like · Comment

 Ming Chan likes this

Ming Chan Michael Jackson.

Tan Hui Lian Hard Rock Cafe.

Excellent American P.R. Endorsed by rock star paraphernalia. Simultaneously, it reinforces the legendary status of American and British music, and the sacred value of all of its debris. Establishes American mythology and legend, as well as ludicrous menu prices. Glorious exotic sounding cuisine, like Buffalo wings, jacket potatoes, poppers and steaks.

Amy Lo Levi's.

Royson Hu Batman!

Despite its subversive anti-hero, Batman was one of the many movies that promoted American preeminence. Gotham-City, based on New York was complete with a magnificent hero who sacrificed everything to protect the integrity of his beloved city. He also boasted a wealthy high status lineage, a beautiful white girlfriend and even a servile Englishman.

Sandra Chan Mickey Mouse.

Coco Tan Beverly Hills 90210.

Beverly Hills 90210 exported the rules of American decorum. It is important to make pointed, cynical assertions. And to be sarcastic. It is often neccessary to humble other people. It is important to be attractive and popular.

*Popular doesn't mean friendly and well-liked. It means being aesthetically, financially and sexually superior to everyone else.

mean sarcastic last word!

humbled silence.

cynical jaded remark!

appreciative laugh.

"America" was the source of glamour and power. If we believed our cinemas, radios and billboard commercials, it was the only source of anyth

At the Convent of the Sacred Heart, Ling Ling was our resident American. She wasn't even American at all, she was said to have spent one year in New Jersey when she was eight years old. But it had been enough for her to learn the American accent, and matched with her undeniable charisma, she was all-powerful.

The Name

Ling Ling's last name was Han, which, if you pronounce it traditionally, rhymes with "fun". But Ling Ling preferred to preserve the name that she had been given in the States, which was a hopelessly mispronounced Han that rhymed with "fan," but in a really long lazy way, sort of like "fayn."

This might not seem like much difference, but there was really no reason for anyone to open up their vowels as wide as "Hayn", and even just the strain of executing the awkward foreign sound could turn heads in the hallway.

The Music

On special occasions, each class could take turns performing a dance routine in front of the whole school. Some classes did local traditional dances, some did interpretations of popular radio songs. Ling Ling kind of made history by dancing to songs that we had never heard of. They came from America and they were called hip hop.

This was something that never played on our radio stations. We had local language stations, or else our only western station played top forty music that only got as bold as Duran Duran.

Ling Ling's dance number shook with the most seductive, provocative rhythm and bass lines our convent stage had ever witnessed. It wasn't that we became immediately intoxicated with hip hop, because it didn't have any context in our lives. We were mainly in awe of its messenger.

Was Ling Ling a good dancer? Now I can't even remember. I just remember that we worked ourselves into a feverish swoon while she gyrated in front of her backup dancers, and pushed it, pushed it good.

highly
uncoordinated
backup
dancers
←......

The Jeans

Everybody noticed Ling Ling's
Levi's. This was back in the
time of skinny jeans, the old
time of skinny jeans, even
before the time of flared
jeans. These were skinny
jeans of the nineties.

In any case, most of us didn't
own jeans, because we lived
on a steaming hot island. Also,
we didn't need a lot more
wardrobe options than school
uniforms and pyjamas.

But once a year we were
allowed to come to school in
normal clothes, and while
most of us scoured the local
night markets looking for
mildly flattering bermudas,
Ling Ling showed up wearing
the latest item out of a
magazine spread. I didn't even
understand them, I remember
wondering how she might
have stuffed the ankles into
her shoes. They were beyond
me. They were from the land
of the free.

The Walk

Ling Ling had also picked up some kind of mysterious body language while she was in America. She had a swagger that no one else could pull off. She swayed through the halls like she had a ten-pound gun holster on each hip.

It might have been the power strut of any neighbourhood gangster, but when she matched it with her exaggerated American jowly vowels, it felt just like a visit from Brandon Walsh from the television series Beverly Hills 90210.

Recess

Ling Ling played basketball
and really, that's just
clearly sexy. But she took it
to another level because
nobody played basketball.
We had been colonized by
England, not Canada, and
so we inherited netball,
which is a very graceful
nimble sport where the ball
flies quickly through the air
and never touches the
ground.

But basketball player s
dribble. So when Ling Ling
hit the court there was
suddenly the sound of a
ball furiously smacking the
cement, pumping under
skirts, flexed between
brown legs and other lewd
macho acts. We didn't
know what America was
like, but we imagined that
Ling Ling's basketball court
was a little local American
theatre.

no belt!
totally against
the rules...

Ling Ling was our idol.
It wasn't that we wanted her love.
We wanted to be worthy of her generation.

Memory: Private School Jezebel

Lenelle Moise

From age five to nine, I attend Saint Patrick's School, an esteemed Roman Catholic institution on a grassless hill in Roxbury, Massachusetts. It is the eighties and Roxbury is a section of Boston that most middle-class people would call "the bad part." Here, where there are gangs, graffiti, immigration, and other colorful things, smiley priests and stern nuns walk the streets with the detached but dutiful air of foreign missionaries.

My best friend Ildulce lives in the neighborhood. She has teeth like small white daggers. She has sneaky, pretty brown eyes. She has silky black hair that falls to the middle of her back. She wears a gold cross between bulging collar bones. She screeches all the words to Madonna's *Like a Virgin*. I love her. Every Friday, during recess, she grabs my brown left thumb in her olive-toned fist and drags me off campus, around the corner, to an overstuffed bodega. We marry our quarters and stock up on *Cigarette Gum*, *Now and Laters* and irresistibly gross *Garbage Pail Kids* trading cards.

One afternoon, in the cold beverage aisle, Ilduce argues with me about which one of the sugary neon dyed 25¢ "drinks" in stubby plastic containers tastes better. I like fake grape but she likes fake orange. "You're crazy," she tells me, flashing her charming, sharp grin. "Grape tastes like butt." I am about to stick my tongue out at her when, suddenly, the sweaty man behind the counter starts shouting, "Shit shit shit, not in front of my store!" We follow his gaze to discover two men tangled in an urgent, wordless fist-fight outside. The stronger one repeatedly bangs the pitiful one's jerry-curled head against an abandoned car's windshield. Jerry Curl's contracted back crash-lands into the bodega's window as his attacker takes off. The store owner continues to curse as he dials 911 but, as our patent leather feet scurry past the bloody beaten man, we can already hear sirens approaching. We stuff sweet junk into our illicit brown paper bags. We stuff the paper bags into our bright pink backpacks. We throw our heads back and laugh, terrified.

The teachers at Saint Patrick's are mostly Irish American and Italian American, with deep crow's feet around well-meaning thirty-something-year-old eyes. My classmates are African American, Puerto Rican, Dominican, Trinidadian, and Cape Verdean. Aside from a pale, strawberry blonde girl named Beverly — whose face flushes fuchsia when we nickname her "Shirley Temple" — most of our little faces are various shades of brown. Only the African American kids comfortably and confidently identify as "black."

Haitian students also attend Saint Patrick's but few are willing to admit their roots. It is the eighties and Haitians in America are dubbed Boat People, even if they crossed the border on a plane, like me. Scientists, comedians, and politicians blame us (and the Harvey Milk-like men of San Francisco) for AIDS. One morning, in kindergarten, a new boy named Christopher joins our class. It is the middle of the school year. He is a handsome, big-butt prince with almond-shaped eyes, puffy cheeks and smooth, dark skin. He is a friendly, albeit nervous, only child who cannot stop talking about his mother. After I catch my first whiff of the spicy clove cologne smell emanating from his talcum-powdered neck, I am determined to develop a crush on him. But then Ildulce suspiciously demands, "Christopher — where are you from?" He honestly replies "Haiti" to which she cries "Eeew!" and for the rest of the school year, he's screwed. Kids call him "Cootie Boy," even though he has the best hygiene in our class. My proud, Haitian parents would be appalled. I never tease Christopher but I also never come to his defense. I steal hellos and goodbyes to him before and after school, palming his back when no one is watching. I tell my friends that I am from Tahiti, an island that sounds like Haiti, an island I cannot begin to locate on a map.

Our principal is Mother Superior. Her other claim to fame is that she is the aunt of popular teen movie star Anthony Michael Hall. He is the unlikely heartthrob featured in *Sixteen Candles, The Breakfast Club* and *Weird Science*. In her office, Mother Superior keeps a gold framed eight-by-ten glossy photo of her famous, scrawny relative beneath an oil painting of Jesus. Anthony (Anthony Michael?) grins like the rich in his studio portrait. Contrastingly, the wide-eyed, melancholy Christ — surrounded by cute but useless cherubs — tilts his bearded chin toward the sky with a look that knows he's about to die. Both nephew and Savior have blonde hair and blue eyes. My principal shares these features but she is chubby with wrinkles. Her gaze is ice.

In the third grade, I am sent to her poorly lit office on four separate occasions: 1) When my mother forgets it is a Half Day and doesn't pick me up on time after school. 2) When my mother forgets to give me $15 for a class field trip to see *The Nutcracker* ballet but sends me to school anyway. 3) When my mother remembers the money for a class field-trip to Rocky Point Amusement Park but forgets that I am supposed to go in my street clothes, not my uniform. And 4) when my mother forgets to have my uniform dry-cleaned and I spend a Monday in an outfit I have already outgrown. On this fourth and most humiliating occasion, the buttons on my sky blue button-down shirt keep popping off and when I sit on my cold classroom seat, my check plaid skirt barely covers my behind. The hard edge of the seat digs into my thighs and leaves an itchy temporary dent to mark where a proper skirt should end. My friends avoid and whisper about me throughout our entire first period. Even Ildulce snickers. When Mr. Balsamo finally writes a note and sends me off into the dim, empty hallways, I am relieved to dodge the critical eyeballs of Catholic school children.

In her office, Mother Superior loudly lectures me about modesty and proper Christian code. Her cold spittle lands on my face as she scolds, "Your skirt should sit past your knees, not in the middle of your thighs! Do you realize that you are distracting your classmates, your teacher! We cannot have you parading the halls like a fallen woman!"

The way she says it, *woman* sounds like the dirtiest word. It resounds without the innocence and sweetness of "little girl" which, because I am tall for my age, is all I really want to be called. *Woman* has a *man* overtly chasing her tail. *Woman* means adult and adults do nasty things children are not supposed to do, like have sex. *Fallen woman* is even worse. I imagine myself tripping on a crack in the pavement, hitting the ground with a thunderous thud, flashing my panties to old ogling bums as my fingers clutch bent, scraped knees. *Fallen woman.* As Mother Superior's chapped lips batter on, I feel bloody from my graceless collapse. I silently wish for oversized clothes that will sag around my frame like a potato sack. Then, holding back tears, I beg her to let me spend the day in her office so as not to cause further disruption back in class. "I swear to God, I'm not a slut!" I plead.

Somehow, my blasphemy calms her. "There, there, my child."

She pets my well-coifed head, "I know this isn't your fault. We shall call your mother immediately to have her pick you up." I wonder who else she is speaking for when she uses the word *We*. I glance up at the images of the famous nephew and the framed Son of Man. She continues, "We certainly cannot keep you in my office much longer, looking like a little Jezebel." I do not know who Jezebel is but the hard *z* and *b* of the name sounds bad. I cross my legs and nod in agreement. Ashamed, I am ready to go home.

While I wait for my mother to pick me up, I ask Mother Superior questions about Anthony Michael Hall. "Does he live in Boston?" "Is he Catholic?" "When did he start acting?" She loves talking about her relative, the 1980s Hollywood star. I do not retain her answers but feel triumphant to have changed the subject and brightened her mood.

When my mother finally arrives, frazzled from having to declare an emergency at work, the head nun passive-aggressively punishes her with words: "Lenelle is suspended for three days. Hopefully, in this time, you can arrange for clean clothes?"

In the car, I burst into tears. My mother grows livid. She shouts, "Who does that bitch think she is?" and I am surprised and elated to hear her swear. She vows to pull me out of Saint Patrick's for good. She tells me as soon as we get home, she is going to call Cambridge Public Schools and see about having me enrolled. "The schools in Cambridge are good, not like Boston. Harrington Elementary is just two blocks away. I would not have to drive you all the way to Roxbury everyday. You could walk to school, like a big girl." She adds that since she won't have to pay private school tuition anymore, we will be able to afford a shopping spree at the mall. "You won't have to wear that ugly navy blue uniform. We'll give them all away. I'll buy you pants and sweaters like Rudy Huxtable wears on *The Cosby Show*. Forget navy blue. You can wear pink and red and green —"

129

"And purple?" I interrupt, thrilled by the promise of new fashion.

"And purple, yes — any color you want." With that, we high-five and I cannot remember walking into Saint Patrick's ever again. In this moment, my mother is my knight, my hero, my savior.

Mama Bird

Myriam Gurba

Mother-to-Be

I really want a human to grow inside of me, but if I put the phone up to my ovaries, you can hear the time for that running out. Tick-tock, tick-tock goes my baby-making clock. Someday, I will christen my child with a traditional Mexican name like Cuidado Piso Mojado. For short, we'll call him Mojado.

Did You Really Think I'd Name My Baby Caution Wet Floor or Wetback? Here Are the Baby Names I'm Considering For Reals

Cuauhtémoc

Moctezuma

Huitzilopochtli

Tezcatlipoca

Tepezcuintle

Hatshepsut

Thoth

Borislav

Bob

Away with Words

For a living, my brother does things with computers. Last week, after he went to a programming conference, he came over. We went out for Chinese. Serving him chop suey, I asked, "How was it?"

"There was a whole lot of Asperger's going on."

ComPUTAdora

The Spanish word for computer is a bordello. The Spanish word for heart attack eats beans (infarto). The Japanese word for mouth opens wide for a pap smear.

Kuchi-kuchi-coo!

Would you let strangers say that to your baby?

If Gabriel Garcia Márquez Mated with John Steinbeck, They Would Name Their Baby A Thousand Years in Vacaville

My Mexican great grandma loved tacos de sesos, beef brain folded into corn tortillas. I think of this intelligent delight as eating computer since brains are basically mushy hard drives. Cow brains compute where the juiciest grasses grow and where oak trees cast superior shade. Grass-fed software decomposed in my great grandma's gastric juices. Moo-cho smart food.

Mad Cow

On TV, I often see forensic psychologists alleging that a serial killer decided to strangle women and eat their brains because he found out his sister was his mother on the same day that he got whacked in the head during a stick ball game gone awry. Well, I fell off the changing table when I was a month old, smacked my head, was nursed by my grandma who's also my aunt, and look at me.

Ancient Aztec Remedy for AIDS

Vicks VapoRub

A Oaxacan Lady Names Her Baby the Most Beautiful Name She's Ever Heard

Alka Seltzer

My Yearbook Superlative

Daughter of the PTA's Hottest Border-hopping MILF

What Would You Have to Do

to win the Aileen Wuornos

Memorial Scholarship Fund?

Be a psychopath?

Be real ugly?

Eat pussy because you have to?

Live in the Everglades?

Wrestle gators?

Keep a comb in your back pocket?

Raise man-hating to an art form?

Promise to take women's studies seriously?

Promise never to show remorse?

Promise to proudly take your throne in hell

Beside a toothless dyke Persephone?

Hatchery

Near TJ's Mustang's bumper, a dead starling curls on her side. Her eyes are shut. Ants crawling over her make her look as if she's vibrating.

I walk to our guava tree to notify her next of kin. Leaning on its trunk, I snoop through branches. Amid tropical green leaves, nestled near a cluster of bulbous fruits, three motherless eggs break my heart. I scoop them up in my palm and carry them inside.

"What's most like a nest?" I think while heading to our bedroom. I slide out of my boxer shorts and let them fall to the wood floor. I climb into bed. My head rests against my brown pillow. I nestle the three eggs in their new home. Some girls have Brillo Pads. I have a coarse nest. It's my bird womb.

The eggs sit near my clitoris for days. Then, one afternoon, I'm awoken from a nap by, "Tap-tap-tap." They're pecking through! I'm going to be a mother! I watch the eggs crack and tear. Out reach ugly heads with huge eyes, hungry beaks snapping.

I reach for the night crawlers I've been keeping in a jar on my nightstand. I pull one out, drop it in my mouth, chew it, swallow it, regurgitate it, and lean my head over my babies. I vomit into their mouths. My breasts, heavy with milk, leak.

Once they grow fat, it's time to fly. I put my children in a pewter cup and carry them to the driveway. I fling my children into the air and one takes off like an eagle, I'm so proud, but another sails too low and the neighbor's pit bull flicks out his tongue and swallows it. This pit bull is a dick. He has already eaten an elotero (corn man) and two paleteros (popsicle men). He has designs on the black mailman.

"Crash!" Another child collides with a windshield. He splatters.

Only the strongest soars. I hope he won't forget me on Mother's Day.

Art Show

Cassie J. Snieder

French Drag Queens, My New Best Friends

Ben McCoy

Since the Harry Winston jewelry heist in Paris on December 4th, 2008, the world has been buzzing about what has been called the largest thievery of its kind, perhaps in the history of France. Representatives have reported the stolen earrings, necklaces, watches, and other jewels were worth a total of $108 million (85 million Euro). But what excites me the most is that three of the four armed robbers were in drag. Whether or not they are on hormones, full-time or part-time transgendered ladies, or at all involved in cabaret or lounge-acts has not yet been confirmed.

Being a shady lady is part DNA, part learned survival skill for drag queens, so it should come as no surprise that these queens have not yet been caught. FINALLY, I'm so proud of my people! Though the 2003 Showtime movie *Soldiers' Girl*, which told the real-life tragic events of Calpernia Adam's life, and the origins of "Don't Ask, Don't Tell," was a monumental and well done representation of a translady's story, the Oscar nominated *Transamerica*, still had the nerve to cast a genetic female, Desperate Actress Felicity Huffman, to portray the leading transgendered lady. In case you're finding it hard to discern my tone here, I found this incredibly lame. Regardless of Huffman's performance, when will Hollywood cast a transgendered lady in a role that requires more than being a cheap punchline in a SNL "man-in-a-dress" sketch?

Investigators believe that the three out of four armed robbers used drag as a way to cloak their identity, and are in fact an arm of an organized group of criminals like the ones portrayed in *Ocean's Eleven*. I choose not to believe this. First of all, no drag queen I know would even be able to sit through twenty minutes of *Ocean's Eleven*. "Actress" Julia Roberts is just not giving enough for any fierce queen to project themselves onto. Second, I'm insulted that investigators think drag queens aren't organized enough to commit such a crime. Because of the rampant trans and homophobia that we live in, queens face discrimination daily. Finding a job that doesn't involve selling drugs or tail is difficult to come by. Straight people are finally getting a taste of what it's been like for transpeople for decades: its *always* a recession for a drag queen. I also question whether or not any of these investigators have ever been to a cabaret show. Do they know how much attention to detail and organization it takes to correctly apply weave-glue to your eyelids, gently gluing a pair of false eyelashes to the tip, arching a flawless brow-line, not to mention applying the concealer, base, foundation, blush, shadow, contouring, highlighter, and setting powder to one's face? YOU spend five years working at a tranny bar lipsynching for straight people and bridal parties, leaping over plastic blow-up penis hats in four-inch stiletto-heeled shoes for thirty dollars of the door and wrinkled up dollar bills shoved in your Fredericks of Hollywood water-bra and you'll soon be devising plans for jewelry heists with your drag queen friends, too! Oh, and the other guy who wasn't in drag? Clearly, he's the hair and makeup guy. Every good queen needs a drag-hag.

Experts say the burglars will have a hard time selling or trading the stolen items legitimately due to their luxurious nature. Again, this is just silly. When was the last time you ever heard of a drag queen doing anything legitimate? Besides, performing in the drag circuit is fiercely competitive. As soon as a new music video appears on YouTube or a new photo appears of a pop diva, queens leap like crazed hyena's to the M.A.C. counter, fabric stores, and sewing machine to perfect their onstage impersonation. And some tired, played-out bangles from Claire's Accessories is just not enough bling to top off your Look. Obviously these French queens are ambitious, goal-driven performers who have that "competitive edge." And here we Americans have been calling the French lazy for years!

While French officials are investigating the whereabouts of the jewels, they really should be patronizing the cabaret bars like Les Folies Bergère, to see a cheap bejeweled crown being given on-stage to a sly winning pageant queen with a neckline drenched in Harry Winston's finest. Though judging from the intelligence of these gender outlaws, I figure they'll be taking at least a six-month hiatus from lip-synching.

As most queens are, I imagine these particular shady ladies were inspired by Madonna — who is after all, the queen of stealing everything. Should the gang of four choose to hide out in the States, I do hope they at least have a real cute weekend stay in San Francisco. They are more than welcome to hide out at my place, as we complain about flesh-toned panty hose over coffee and eggs, and bitterly confess our romantic woes. Employment isn't the only area of discrimination for transladies, as romance takes the cake for unfair treatment. After dealing with a lifetime of heterosexual men who only want a discreet, behind-hotel-doors "NSA" sexual relationship with a lady-with-something-extra, some Harry Winston jewelry seems an expensive consolation prize. Together my new-found outlaw friends and I would sigh over the fact that H. W. doesn't make luxury clip-on earrings, as we'd pose together with one another for photos I'd later post on Facebook under the title "French Drag Queens, My New Best Friends."

Some of you may have wildly misinformed ideas of why such a heist occurred. On top of the phobia and discrimination that trans people face, we are also constantly expected to be "FIERCE," "FLAWLESS," and "FASHION-FORWARD" — which is not cheap, girlfriend. Have you ever considered the cost of laser hair removal to your face, neck, torso, arms, legs, fingers, toes, teeth, personality, and bedding? And though the illegal purchasing of hormone shots may be considerably cheaper, sharing needles hasn't really been trendy since the mid-80s. Don't even get me started on trachea shaving (the reduction of the Adam's Apple), and other plastic surgeries, as I find them problematic. And don't think such treatments and lavish bank-breaking procedures are purely vanity: for a translady, "passing," (being read by the people who surround you as a female) helps ensure your physical safety in a world where hate crimes still happen. Transladies are still being murdered, beaten, and stabbed for the expression of their identity. The promise of cosmetic enhancements is not only a reflection of one's vanity, but, for transladies, one step closer to potentially avoiding physical harm. Suddenly, the desperation and conniving needed to perform such a highly organized robbery isn't so far-fetched.

from Yokohama Threeway

Beth Lisick

Dog Towel

There is a time in your life when you start becoming a guest in other people's homes. These people are seldom married, but are more likely a couple who is living together for the first time, which feels exotic because they don't have any housemates or anything. Like there is no guy named Craig or Domino renting the small storage room under the stairs who plays Neil Young songs on the guitar at night when he can't sleep. Either that, the Neil songs, or it's just unrestrained, balls-out sobbing.

These couple-friends say to you, *Come up to Portland anytime. We are renting a great little bungalow while Jody is getting her Masters in Public Health.*

And no one has any babies yet. Babies are like phantom demons at this time in your life and you are sure that only the most boring and conventional among you will ever have them. Babies smell horrible and cramp your style. Babies are the ultimate paradox; born so that you can start to die. These people, your friends, are well on their way to having one of their own. Therefore, the stench of death is fully hovering over Jody and Dave. They are about twenty-six or twenty-seven. Old.

How interesting the way some people live, you think in their tiled foyer as you examine a coat rack featuring carved kokopellis, those little humpbacked Native American guys who play the flute. And look at the pristine bathroom with its blinding grout and bounty of clean towels folded on the freestanding rattan shelves. The towels are an explosion of primary colors. As if to make drying off a celebration. As if they're saying, *Hey, do you party? I heard you like to party.*

The cool water will feel good after a day spent in a Winnebago on the interstate. Separate the folds of the shower curtain, a see-through vinyl one except for the parts where there is a colorful map of the world. Look at all that ocean hanging around and you've barely been anywhere.

After shutting off the shower, your eye moves to another stack of towels on the shelf below. These towels are grayish and beigeish and thinnish. There are about ten of them. A lot. Grab one of those instead. The humble ones.

But now smell your naked body. You used a quarter-sized dollop of the Pink Grapefruit Body Wash, but your skin reeks musty and barfy and you are matted with the short black hairs from Lucky. Lucky, who greeted your arrival today in the traditional snout-in-the-vagina style.

Later, when you are dressed, your friend brings you and the other five houseguests into the bathroom and gestures at the two stacks of towels. He is making a performance of it.

"All I'm saying is what kind of person looks at those two stacks of towels . . . and then uses *those*? Who among you would do that?"

Everyone laughs while you clamp your jaw down hard like you're biting off more of that buffalo jerky from the Winnemucca gas station.

"Those just looked like your nice towels so I didn't want to use them," you say.

"Yeah, they're our nice towels. They're the towels we put out for guests in our house," he says. "Towels for people."

Yokohama Threeway

Which movie star do you look like? That's a game that Japanese people used to like to play with white people in the early nineties. I don't know if they play it anymore now that white people and movie stars are easier to view on your computer than ever before, but the best one I ever got: Babala Stleisandu.

I was hoping the old man at the ramen house meant the *What's Up Doc?* Babala Stleisandu as opposed to the *Prince of Tides* Babala Stleisandu, but everyone covered their mouths and made high-pitched noises of lite embarrassment. One lady even tried to make me feel better by saying it was only because of my nose. That was all. Just like Barbra in the nose.

Now, Jodie Foster. She was who my friend got all the time. And something about the fact that I was in Japan made me not care about being the Yentl to her Clarice Starling. Really most of the month in Yokohama was spent with a similar sort of not caring much about whatever was happening, in alternately glorious and insidious ways. For instance, I was eating stinky tofu and wearing mismatched socks a lot, things I never did back home. Plus lying around naked in close proximity of my naked friend and her naked manfriend.

Such a dirty bird, he was. Where did he get off anyway? Wait, I know this one. Right on my face, apparently. In my eye.

Which leads me to a tiny Q & A.

Q: What do you call a middle-aged British man who has been living in Japan for fifteen years and has yet to learn to speak the language?

A: A pervert.

Q: What is wrong with being a pervert?

A: Nothing.

Q: Why are you being a jerk then?

A: Sometimes it just seems like there are a lot of dudes who are into plaid skirts and coming on your face.

Q: So pedestrian versions of "nonconformity" make you agitated?

A: Burning Man syndrome. Sometimes I lash out.

That first night at dinner he was okay. Said I reminded him of a cat, which I think was supposed to be a compliment, but that is just judging from Halloween costumes that grown women wear. But in the middle of my inaugural threeway, on a futon in a room with rice paper doors and a tatami mat, it hit me. I was one of two California girls, fresh out of college, currently doing it with a weird older guy. In Japan even. The mysterious land of sexual pleasure. Bang a gong.

Straddling one or the other, I thought, Huh, so when the last of bit of my flesh chars in the crematorium, I will have been a woman who helped a mediocre man live out a classic scenario from Penthouse Forum.

A bigger problem is that this guy had a method for drying off after a shower that he enjoyed sharing with new friends. Before you reach for the towel, sort of squeegee yourself with the palm of your hand first. Squeegee down the length of one arm, shake off the water, and then the other, shake off the water, then down one leg, shake off the water, and then the other. Shake off the water. The point is to save your towel from getting soaked. This actually ended up proving useful in later years when living in damp, cave-like apartments where there was no natural light and a thin coating of mold crept rapidly upon my shoe leather.

I still think of him just after turning off the shower, right before I reach for the towel. And then for some reason that triggers the following thought: I bet somewhere out there is a cat named Barbra Streisand.

The False Imprisonment Fiasco

Let's go around to the side of the house. Let's do it back there. It's only dirt piles and pool equipment and a patch of mustard greens that my brother planted. They were too bitter for anyone to eat and now they're dead. We'll use that tree in the corner. It's strong enough to hold her if we tie the rope tight enough. Did you get the rope from the garage? Okay, now you hide behind the gate so when she opens it she won't know you're here. I'll try to get her to go over near the tree and that's when you come out. Once she sees you just keep going toward her until we have her backed up against the tree and then we'll use the rope. Oh no. We need a scarf to tie around her mouth so no one can hear her scream. In my mom's closet. Hurry. There's one with colored polka dots. She'll come right across Titus Avenue from her dirty house that always smells like syrup where the sad, fat mom is trying to raise five kids after the dad left her for someone else who we have never seen. He thinks he is so great in that green Audi Fox. With his golf clubs and tennis racket and bald head. And then the mom went and got super into Jesus and now they all go to that weird huge church on the other end of the valley that people call a superchurch. All of them except for the redhead brother who is mean, mean, mean. Shannon's the skinny twin, the one that popped out second, the cute one who doesn't stutter and can do good cartwheels. She will stay tied up to this tree until everyone is worried about her, whenever that will be, and she will cry and she will pay. No one warps my Grease soundtrack album and gets away with it. Looking through a knothole in a fence always makes my eye burn.

from **Black Wave**

Michelle Tea

Mary Kay Letourneau! Ziggy shrieked, clipping her in the shoulder with their shared 40-oz.

What? Michelle cried. She's Eighteen! That's Legal!

Mary Kay Letourneau, Ziggy repeated, shaking her head. They moved together through the darkness of South Van Ness, passing Victorians protected from the street by wild shrubbery and tall iron fences. The overhang of trees blotted the street lights, and the sidewalk was empty of people. In the coming blocks hookers would suddenly materialize, women in big shoes and cheap little outfits. Sometimes Michelle would be walking alone in a similar outfit and the women would regard her skeptically, wondering if she was working their block. Men in cars would slow their roll, also inquisitive. Michelle offered smiles of solidarity to the females and flipped off the men, masking her fear with snobbish indignation, praying for them to drive away. Once, drunk, she removed a high heel and walked toward the curb as threateningly as one can in such a gait, one pump on, one pump held menacingly above her head. The man drove away. Mostly the men were simply looking to purchase sex, not terrorize anyone. Michelle understood that to truly support a prostitute meant wishing her a successful business, and this meant streets teeming with inebriated men propositioning anyone who looked slutty from their car windows. She tried to have a good attitude about it.

Michelle wrenched the 40 from her friend's grip. She hated sharing anything with Ziggy. Ziggy bogarted the booze, and her strangely wet lips soaked cigarette filters. Once Michelle hit her Camel Light only to have Ziggy's saliva ooze from the spongy tip. Ziggy would not take a languid, gentle inhalation, but a stressed-out trucker pull, one and then another, making the cigarette hot, the tip a burning cone. Michelle did not know what to do with such a cigarette. She would rather buy Ziggy a carton of Camels than share a smoke with her, but she was stuck. Ziggy was her best friend, and everyone was broke.

Ziggy was both scandalized and delighted by Michelle's love-at-first sight encounter with the teenaged slam poet. Her walk when newly drunk became a sort of dance, she swiveled out from her hips as she slid down the street. Like many butches, Ziggy dealt with her feminine hips by weighing them down with a lot of junk. A heavy belt was threaded through the loops of her leather pants. The word RAGGEDY was spelled in metal studs across the back, as if you could not simply see for yourself. All the dykes had recently discovered the shop in the Castro where leather daddies got their belts and vests and caps and chaps. A bearded fag resembling the Greek god Hephaestus would pound the word of your choice into the leather with bits of metal. It was expensive, but worth it if you had it. Ziggy went from rags to riches regularly, scoring jobs at Yuppie restaurants and then slipping on a wet floor and throwing her back out. She blew her cash on leather goods and rounds of tequila for everyone, plus some cocaine and maybe a nice dinner in a five-star restaurant where service people treated her like swine.

Whatever was left over was given away to people on the street, and then it was back to bumming cigarettes off her friends.

But, Ziggy's hips: a Leatherman was snapped to the belt, like a Swiss Army knife but more so. The gadget flipped open into a pair of pliers with a world of miniature tools fanning out from the handles. Screwdriver, corkscrew, scissors, tweezers. The Leatherman was a lesbian phenomena and life ran more smoothly because of it. Ziggy had that on one hip and a buck knife in a worn leather sheath on the other. A hankie forever tufted from her back pocket, corresponding to the infamous faggot hankie code. The hue, pattern or even the textile flagging from Ziggy's ass transmitted the desire for a particular sexual activity; right or left pocket communicated whether the butch would prefer the giving or receiving end. Ziggy's tastes were varied and shifting, and hankies of many sort danced between her cheeks. That night a flash of lamé dangled from her right ass pocket, signaling her wish to be fucked by a fancy femme.

In Ziggy's other pocket sat a leather wallet, hooked to her belt loop with a swag of silver chain. Nights that Ziggy packed, yet another layer of leather and metal would be rigged across her hips, a heavy dildo curled in her underwear. The overall effect of these accessories was not unlike a woman dancing hula in a skirt of shells and coconuts, or bellydancers draping their bellies in chain mail. The swinging, glinting hardware propelled Ziggy forward from her core, and though your eyes were drawn to the spectacle, like dazzle camouflage, the flash obscured the femininity. A lot of butches wore this look, but Ziggy did it best.

Gay Men Fuck Younger Boys All The Time, Michelle said fiercely. *Okay, NAMBLA*, Ziggy snorted. *Okay, NAMBLA Kay Letourneau.*

Not Like *That*, Michelle said. Just — You Know What I Mean. Older Fags And Younger Fags, Like *Legally* Young. Daddies. Zeus And Ganymede. *Ganymede was a child*, Ziggy schooled.

Yeah, You Were There, Michelle retorted. On Mount Olympus. You Were Working The Door. You Carded Ganymede. Michelle's joke reminded her of a true story, in which Ziggy picked up a girl with hair so short there was almost nothing for her Hello Kitty barrettes to clamp onto. She wore a pink dog collar around her neck and left her ID on Ziggy's bedroom floor by accident. She hadn't been old enough to get into the bar where Ziggy seduced her.

That's not the same thing, Ziggy defended. *That girl lied to me. Just by being in the bar she was pretending to be at least twenty-one. That was not my fault.*

So, she said, If That Poet Lied To Me About Her Age It Would Be Okay? *It's Too Late,* Ziggy said scornfully, swigging the Old English. *You Met Her At The Teen Poetry Slam. It Is Too Late For You, NAMBLA Kay Letourneau.* Ziggy's hips swiveled as she skipped along. She sashayed down the block, nearly running into a shriveled old crackhead woman who had emerged from the mouth of an SRO Hotel. At least Michelle thought she was old. She might have been thirty but crack is such an evil potion, it turned maidens to hags in a season.

You know what to do!!!! The woman croaked in a prophetic timbre. *Do it! Do! It! Do it now! Do it now!* Michelle and Ziggy looked at one another, alarmed. Lifelong city dwellers, both were accustomed to the spooky public outbursts of addicts and crazy people, but Ziggy tended to treat them as oracles dispensing coded messages.

Do what?! Ziggy asked, suddenly desperate. *Do what?! Oh, God! I feel like that woman just looked into my soul!* Ziggy's eyes got the focused unfocused look that only a drunk Pisces with eyes that color green could achieve. She retraced her steps and pulled a palmful of coins from the tight front pocket of her leather pants. She placed it in the woman's chickeny hand.

You know, she told Ziggy. A bright piece of her fabric wound around her head, and her eyes stared out from the cave of her face *You know!*

I do, Ziggy replied solemnly. *Thank you.*

Michelle thought Ziggy was probably crazy herself, but there was a chance she wasn't, and that the street people of her neighborhood were in fact prophets, apocalyptically wise, witches born into a time of no magic. Michelle preferred this story over the alternative of everyone having chemical imbalances and genetic predispositions toward alcoholism. She supported Ziggy and helped her puzzle out the cryptic warning of the street oracle.

Is There Anything You Think You Should Do Right Now? Michelle asked. Ziggy thought.

Write a novel? She mused. Ziggy stuck to poetry, but it was hard to make money as a poet and Ziggy really liked money. Another option was moving to Los Angeles to direct films but that seemed like such an intense thing to do. *Apply for a grant?* She dug deep. *I was thinking about doing yoga*, she said. Recently Ziggy had been on brief dates with a bi-curious yoga instructor who kicked everyone's ass at pool. *Prana*, the girl smiled after sinking the final ball, raising her fingers to the barroom ceiling in a spiritual gesture.

You Want To Do Some Yoga And Improve Your Pool Game? Michelle asked. One of the errant ways Ziggy brought in extra cash was pool sharking. Another was shining shoes with an old-fashioned shoe shine kit she lugged from bar to bar like a butch version of those Peachy Puff girls selling cigarettes and candy and useless light-up plastic roses. As the Peachy Puffs wore ridiculous and sexy costumes resembling the spangled outfits little girls tap dance in, Ziggy knew which garments would appropriately fetishize her labor. She shined shoes in a stained wife-beater and a tight pair of Levi's.

Maybe She Was Talking To *Me?* Michelle suggested. Do It, Like, Make Out With The Poet.

The teen, Ziggy corrected.

Lucretia, Michelle insisted. But the name was such a mouthful. Was it her real name, she wondered. San Francisco was full of people who changed their names upon moving to town. Trashbag, Spike, Monster, Machine, Scout, Junkyard, Prairie Dog, Flipper, Fiver, Kiki, Smalley, Rocks, Carrot, Rage, Sugar, and Frog were only some of the individuals Michelle had met since coming to California. *I Don't Think You Should Do It,* Ziggy said.

The thing was, Michelle already had a girlfriend. Her last name was Warhol, so everyone called her Andy, though the name on her driver's license was Carlotta. Andy was on a lesbian soccer team. Michelle liked to watch her spike the ball with her head like an aggressive seal. Andy cooked meals at an AIDs Hospice in the Castro. She was older than Michelle and had been doing this for many, many years, had been through the terrible era when gay men were dying and dying and dying and dying. Michelle had assumed Andy prepared healthful, nourishing, life-prolonging foods for these men, but as they all had death sentences what she did was cook them their last meals, again and again. Pork chops, ribs, mashed potatoes, mac and cheese, fried chicken. Hamburger Helper when it was requested, and it was. Meat loaf. Cupcakes and brownies and pies with ice cream. Andy fed Michelle, too. It was a foundation of their relationship, without Andy there were many times when Michelle would have gone hungry, so broke and unemployable was she, so hell-bent on prioritizing liquor above food. Wasn't beer bread, Michelle asked in earnest? Liquid bread? Especially Guinness, didn't they give Guinness to pregnant women in some country, Ireland she supposed, and wasn't Michelle Irish, didn't years of ethnic evolution give her a genetic gift for absorbing the nutrients in a pint of beer?

Generally, people who did not drink like Michelle — let's call it heavily — generally, they would not want to date her. It was unusual how Andy not only accepted Michelle's inebriation, but encouraged it. She bought jugs of beer beyond Michelle's normal price range. She procured pills from folks at work and urged Michelle to take them. This dynamic inspired in Michelle a variety of emotion. Sometimes she felt like a helpless princess being caretaken by a handsome butch. Andy was black Irish which was some mythological breed of Irish caused by the mating of the natives with a boatful of Iberians, producing people who looked like Andy — white as a ghost with a head full of black, black hair. When Andy was a little girl she prayed to unicorns to not get boobs, and it worked. Her black hair fell into a natural superman swirl on her forehead. Andy was attractive in the manner of an old-fashioned movie star, Michelle thought, or maybe it was her chivalry, if chivalry was what it was. Sometimes Michelle worried that Andy just wanted to knock her out so that she didn't have to deal with talking to or fucking her. Michelle tended to never shut up, and she wanted big drama in bed all the time, requiring her lover to be a roller coaster or tsunami.

Michelle and Andy were not faithful to one another. Theirs was a messily open relationship, one in which the rules and boundaries were never fully articulated so could never be fully broken. In spite of this, there was the *feeling* that Michelle was shitting on the rules all the time with her haphazard acquisition of lovers. She had an affair with a junkie troubadour named Penny, who sang Johnny Thunders songs on her acoustic guitar as they walked through the industrial wasteland of her neighborhood. Dogpatch, a place not yet gentrified, with vacant storefronts and SRO hotels, one of which Penny lived in. Penny had tangled black hair that clawed out from her head like Medusa. She wore spandex pants and clunky boots with broken zippers. The boots barely stayed on her feet so there was always the exciting possibility that Penny would wipe out. Walking down the street with her was like watching a circus acrobat. Penny's small room was padded with thrift store clothing, mounds of it. They made out on a mattress on the floor, a muted black and white television strobing them with *Nosferatu*.

In the morning panic woke Michelle like an alarm clock. Who was this elegant skeleton she was curled into? This hair had a new smell, a dusty stink of Aqua Net Super Extra Hold, also a drugstore perfume worn as a joke, and also dirt, and sweat, and the tang of heroin — brown sugar and spoiled wine. Though Penny was who she'd wanted last night, slow kisses tasting of new intoxicants, Andy was who she wanted to wake up with, the shore she longed to beach herself upon.

Michelle peered through makeup-crusted eyes at the thrift store clothes heaping the walls in dunes — they would be smothered in an earthquake! Penny shambled out of bed, so frail in the daylight, and rutted through the base of a pile, extracting something that shimmered like the scales of a magical fish. She pulled it over her torn nightgown and left to throw up in the bathroom down the hall. Michelle fled. She wheeled about Dogpatch, an unfamiliar neighborhood, the apocalyptic times that were upon them glaring from every bit of rubble: mounds of festering shit left by packs of wild dogs she hoped she would not run into. Did buses even run out here? How had she arrived? Penny had met her on the corner, with her guitar. She had strummed *You Can't Put Your Arms Around A Memory*, singing it with a cracking voice. Penny really was like the girl Johnny Thunders. Someone had tattooed *Chinese Rock* on her shoulder with a sewing needle. It was a spidery tattoo, the lines shook crooked down her skin, but it worked with her look. Penny was amazing, but Michelle worried there was a time limit on that sort of amazing. That it was the sort of amazing that could begin to look sad with age. Michelle fought against this analysis, which seemed cruel and typical. The messed-up queers Michelle ran with tempted fate daily, were creating a new way to live, new templates for everything — life, death, beauty, aging, art. Penny would never be pathetic, she would always be daring and deep, her addiction a middle finger held up to proper society. Right? Right?

WHERE IS MY SOUL?

By: Cristy C. Road

I was ecstatic over the idea of it--being on Sister Spit tour; the tour that launched a million queers. The tour that presented the voices of distressed and passionate writers of the 90's who, in many ways, changed my entire life. I could not believe that this, in its mature incarnation, would soon be my reality.

Eventually, it was my reality and I had a flight to Seattle at 7pm. I wasn't even ready to leave my house that day. The sweat on my palms seared through every object I touched and I convinced myself it would be impossible to open the front door. I knew that my enthusiasm would be resurrected once I was sitting inside the van; but all I could really think about was the electricity bill, being in the closet to my family, and my broken heart. A broken heart that was hardly broken; just lacking psychotherapy. And in true 24-yr old/ pre-Saturn-Return fashion; I did not feel psychotherapy was necessary at the time.

"God, where is my soul?" I thought to myself, smoking a massive joint. "Where is my enthusiasm and my understanding that I am doing this thing I have always wanted to do?" I thought to myself, as I disguised the homosexual connotations of my forthcoming tour in the news update on my webpage; for the sake of the closet I crawled inside of; using words like "feminist" instead of "queer".

I am an occasionally self-lothing Cuban American woman who
is trudging along the sidelines of bohemian America. I left the
tender sheath of my hometown in order to pursue gayer pastures;
while maintaining closeness with my culture via legitimate Cuban
cuisine, blistering salsa music, holiday visits, daily telephone
calls, and my hair. I decided to grow out all of my hair in order
to feel like La Quinceañera that punk rock and queer visibility
was unable to enable. Despite the radical Latino pastures, fields
of free-love, and metropolitan vortexes that housed my transient
heart year after year; I still felt a daunting void.

APRIL 2007

And so, my new life commenced. I was now confined to a queer van
full of queer authors and queer visibility; but highly adult
tasks. Adult perspectives on being a writer and being an artist

shone through the windowpane;
through our eyes; our pens and
our paper. I nuzzled my insecure
self among my new friends who
profusely sweat inspirational
value. Michelle Tea, Ali
Liebegott, Eileen Myles, Nicole
Georges,
Rhiannon
Argo,
Robin
Akimbo,
Tamara
Llosa
Sandor,
and our
managerial
road
demon:
Annie
Oakley.

Our
first
night was
in
Seattle,
Washington, then Olympia, followed by Portland, Oregon. Annie
maneuvered our titanium road castle along Highway 5 as we fell in
love with inside joke after inside, particularly the casual use of
the term BURL. It took a day or two to wipe off the last few

months' emotional debris. Summer camp is a hard thing you know? Especially when your moon is in Cancer; so at first everything feels alienating and alone. It's a good thing my sun and ascendant are in Gemini, because after 3 days; everyone knew my shit. I believed in us; and I felt less and less like the awkward depressed spectator that got on that flight to Seattle a few days ago.

As soon as we arrived in San Francisco, I thought, "I HAVE ARRIVED". I was performing with Sister Spit in the legendary birthing ground of the punk subgenre that altered my entire life, and allowed me to hail the call of queer pop-punk; whether my parents liked it, or not. The van dropped me off at 24th and Mission to meet with my old friend, Susan. As I saw her car in the distance, I ran towards an unnerving oblivion and tripped my tender size 5 foot on the curb; spraining my ankle in a horrifying fashion. I hardly considered this a sprain, but a biological mutation. I basically wanted to die. There was a giant mound growing out of my ankle and Dr. Lee at The General Hospital was the only person who could ever understand what happened. As Susan held me; I told her about everything--- about the broken heart, the fear of rejection, the fear of abandonment,

the

uncertainty which hovered above me when I acknowledged the disconnect between my identity and my family. Unfortunately, it *was* just a sprain, and I wasted about $200 in medical bills at the General Hospital that could have gone towards 29 bottles of Ibuprofen. I did, however, acquire a fine set of crutches that truly assisted my partial immobility.

The wait at the Hospital went on for 4-5 unbearable hours and I
ended up missing the performance. Upon arriving for the last 20
minutes; everyone embraced me and everyone loved me. Everyone
advised me that they got the crowd to send me positive energy
through telepathic communication. I received that energy----
through Susan and Dr. Lee and later through Susan's large white
dogs whose breed was unfamiliar to me; but whose awkward affection
was unparalleled.

Despite aching limbs, lost love, and unfinished processing;
we carried on. Day after day, affirmation after affirmation, we
performed
our whole selves
out. Although
like any day
like today or
yesterday,
we lived
our lives as
we typically
would. The
best part
of tour is
forgetting
that you are
on tour. One
minute
you're
performing
at a pizza
place in
the southwest
while looking at rock
formations
completely alien to
your northeastern
sensibilities; and the
next minute you're
talking late into the
night with your van-mate,
about the synchronicity between your turbulent lives back home.
Still, I never really asked everyone in the van what I was
thinking when I sunk into my insecurities--- How do you do this?
How do you grow so gracefully, achieving levels of confidence and
success while maintaining your grit and spirit? Your anger and
identity? How do I become Eileen Myles??
I kept the questions to myself and learned via specks of
conversation. All interactions created the belief that we were all

fuck-ups once. We were all drowning in our own version of sorrow, at some point in time. Now, we were all here; hashing out our deepest thoughts and taking ourselves seriously. We were here, we were queer, and we proficiently designed this tour to assure you of that.

I think this was the first time that being in the closet to my family didn't feel isolating or cowardly, but cultural and human.

Every so often, I would wake up amidst a rebirth; as if this wasn't just another tour of writers or artists or punk rock bands, but a catalyst to the rest of my life.

In Las Vegas we had a hot tub in the hotel and Annie missed the show because she won tickets to see Roseanne Barr. In new England, Ali rescued a lonely duck and performed with her on stage. In Chicago I fell in love 4 or 5 times with both people and buildings so I made a note to self about coming back. In Ohio I sat outside on a bench in the parking lot and cried on the telephone for over an hour; but Michelle wore a pair of heels that sparkled like the starry canvas that was the sky that night. On Route 66 we found charming roadside attractions and

kept that charm with us until we retreated to a cabin upstate and
watched The Craft (starring Faruza Balk) in our pajamas. From
coast to coast; we spoke about our "fucked up lives" in spaces
that were reserved for education. Adulthood crept up beside me in
the hallways of William and Mary, Ohio State, Bard, and whatever
nameless or prestigious U of GAY would take
us. Resilience from the last month
settled at every bookstore or
dive bar.

This was not the Sister Spit I
read about; but the product of
what could happen when you
spend your entire life
toiling in passionately
impractical conditions for
the sake of making art. I had
spent my life doing so;
reaping the solace, the
damage, and the rewards of a
DIY motive, true to class
and true to beliefs.
Although at times I felt
stuck; as if I was speaking
to myself and a few people
who were just like me. No
growth, no inclusion, no
transformation. In the van;
I saw we could do it all---
pay our bills, without
commodifying our struggle or
compromising anything we
need to say.
    In a perfectly cathartic fashion, SISTER SPIT 2007 ended
around Florida; where I would connect with my family before
heading back to my home in Brooklyn.

    Every so often, I want to relive that surge of going from
nothingness to everything in one fell swoop. It wasn't just the
feeling of creating a literary revolution; but the feeling of
reinventing your purpose without a barricade between you and your
identity.

A few months later I came out to my mom.

Then I grew out my entire eyebrow.

High Five for Ram Dass

Harry Dodge

Book 1

"Two of the members are stuck down a hole." Asia has been sent back to find us, perhaps a day and a half behind Group 1. She emerges from a patch of Palo Verde and skips the last few feet down into the wash. We are surrounded by grey rocks the size of bronto-saurus testicles. My ankles are weak. "The Neils think you are the only one who can get him out." I hate all the Neils. Smug, I hate smug. I would never ever name a person Neil after this experience.

Marx the Authoritarian is whimpering by the time I arrive. I guess smack dab in the middle of clubbing a squirrel to death, he started an allergic reaction to an unripe prickly pear they had just finished brunching on. With a muted snap, his epiglottal appendage had very suddenly inflamed to the size of a ping pong ball. Presum-ably, he reeled, lost his footing and was hurled into the old well. As an aside, at approximately twenty-nine inches in diameter it was a ridiculously tight opening and had to have been excavated initially by a real lazy motherfucker.

I notice a trio of scavengers have dragged over a small set of bleachers and I suppose people will be making themselves at home for the duration of the spectacle. One of Marx the Authoritarian's legs is underneath him touching the floor of the damp trap, and one leg is straight above him. His knee is pressing into his throat "really really hard!" he yells up, but his allergic reaction has subsequently reversed itself. And again, I'm not sure how Sabbath died and then got down there on top of him.

"Air Supply, is that you buddy?" The length of the cave actually amplifies his voice. The voice of the clumsy spelunker. "I hope to God that it's you." I can hear that he is drooling.

I get down on all my knees, put my cheek to the warm dirt around the rim of the loamy ventricle. "You've been off-kilter lately," I murmur. I know he can hear me perfectly. A dense hush settles onto the bleachers.

"What? Shit. I'm totally smashed in here man!" His voice cracks. I sit up for a moment and concentrate on a set of deep amber buttes way off to my right. I narrow my eyes at the Neils, who are all puckered together in the front row. M the A is crying now. Apparently subsumed by a panic that strikes me and most of the other people on the bleachers as unattractive. Where was my sportsmanship now? Beyond my control was the urge to crap down the hole instead of just jettison my garbagey thoughts.

Having been on the land the longest (by my count) I was both respected and regarded with suspicion. I had managed to become an outsider among the outsiders (while living outside). Bruised with the psychic arrows discharged continually by the lingering specter of youth culture (you can take the young out of culture . . .), I inarguably remained . . . a being diminutive in physical stature and, more to the point, fundamentally narrow. I also had long hairs that protruded idiotically from both of my nostrils. For these reasons and some others I will refrain from mentioning, I was therefore best qualified for the dangerous mission that was to follow.

"Spirituality is a mean nasty chicken snatcher," I said down the hole. "Spirituality," I tilted my head away from the earthy orifice in a covert address to the remaining bystanders, "no matter how softy soft you think it is — steals the marvelous from the physical world." I was totally off the point and I knew it. A renewed round of sobs arose from the soggy grotto.

"What are you driving at, Air Supply?!" His cries sounded like a dog yelping. I felt like killing him.

"Let's eat him after you pull him up," Neil Sedaka suggested. His tiny flipper fins wriggled almost imperceptibly just off his clavicle.

Neil Sedaka. There was a guy whose surgery had gone well. Amputations, reductions, substitutions were now substantially more commonplace than, say, five years ago. I think in lieu of the lobotomy for lingual excision, aerodynamism was compelling to pretty much everyone who ended up becoming a member. Helen Reddy had once described a related mindset that materialized just after the millennium. They started calling it body integrity identity disorder. Where a person requests an amputation. They have a mulish desire for their body to physically match the idealized image they have of themselves. A very spicy paradox, the idea of losing one or more major limbs on the road to becoming whole. "Less is more," Helen Reddy had chortled. Chicago was always calling it Modernism and then farting.

Book 2

Shortly after I was able to sit up, my mother strapped me to my potty seat and left me there for just over three years. I still have calluses on the back of my thighs to prove it. She managed to feed me now and then, empty the bowl on most days, and wipe me down biennially, but she never said a damn thing in my direction. I was just like a little tunnel. Respirating. Memorizing the lines of the dim doorway, the knob, a glowing yellow shade over my left shoulder. Sometimes I heard her crying, padding around in her slippers, one day she killed a cat in the downstairs foyer. City workers eventually found me there, a little filthy pink Rodin, pooping. I was real skinny. At that point — so the story goes — I wanted to know the words for everything. Humans are funny and stupid. Why would I want to know the words for anything? We have like cookie cutters instead of brains.

I met my one good friend at the Agency, though. There were a lot of feral kids there, or partially feral, but the best one was a kid they rescued off a Patagonian plateau a few years before. He had been in the wilderness there since he was four and half, tending sheep. Enslaved, apparently, and neglected. He never really cared to speak, was barely managing his daily chorus "I'd gladly go back" over a late lunch one day when he keeled over of a brain aneurism. I tried to help him, but I thought he was choking on a French fry and was way into the Heimlich thing when the EMTs showed up and noticed the blood balloon forming on the side of his tender, eager, little enslaved head. I miss him though, don't get me wrong. I can still hear his tiny whispering mantra. Probably he's why I ended up on this land, trying to figure out how to get Marx the Authoritarian out of his hole.

I started submitting articles to the Food Insects Newsletter and the Society for Primitive Technology at the age of thirteen. The first one was called Hunter Gatherers Were Sometimes Very Labor-Efficient. The second one, Collecting Ant Pupae For Food. At sixteen I submitted an incisive piece entitled *They Ate What!?* in italics with a question mark and exclamation point. There were too many to name. My annual Food Insect Festivals of North America garnered me the coveted Leppy in 1989 and Fried Grasshoppers For Campouts Or At Home is to date the one of which I am most proud.

My preludial phases are most effectively characterized by the sentence fragment that follows, "A bunch of ass-eating jumbos." The assorted biological anti-fruits of my failed gene enhancements are — however — at this juncture quite striking and — I have to admit — have garnered a certain amount of praise and/or erotic attention. Chicks dig me. Life as an earthling without outer ear cones, less one arm, and with three spindly little brittle-boned birdlegs has not been as wholly joyless as one (not in the know) may imagine. There are thousands of us. Narrows we're called. Our bodies are more cylindrical (although the difference is negligible and for the most part imperceptible), and our ribs are very flexible.

When it counts, I can fit into places that are most certainly a pretty tight squeeze for the old guard.

Book 3

We are allowed to bring five pounds in with us. Like heredity. Where you show up with a certain load. Primeval gifts we give ourselves. I bring in a very lightweight sleeping bag that frays and disintegrates over the course of my first week. In addition I bring in a stack of pornography which comes in handy as a blanket until I perfect the employment of pine boughs, coal beds and various terrain appropriate shelters.

Chicago, Asia, Fleetwood Mac. We are all given soft rock names as we arrive. The goal is a resynthesis of the worst of contemporary culture. Vaccinations. Sometimes someone gets the name of a person who didn't do soft rock. One guy got the name Lee Iacocca and another guy, his lover, when they came at the same time got Simon Wincer, who directed *Free Willy* in 1993. No one on the land knows who the original Simon Wincer is but Simon Wincer the guy from our group feels okay even not having a famous name to live out the rest of his days with. Another guy got the name Marx the

Authoritarian. Which I thought was nice cuz it rhymed with Conan the Barbarian. He was just a little guy though, like me. He was really nice and kind of wispy.

There's only been one baby born into the community. Eagles and Beegees had a perfect little hermaphrodite which they called The Brown Dwarf. Brown dwarfs are this type of star in actual outer space that never lit on fire. They have a lot of mass but not enough to create the explosion that would light them up. So they account for some of the mass or gravity that certain near galaxies exert but we have no way of seeing them because they do not emit light. They apparently have a sucking capability that does not rival a black hole. It is a brown dwarf. A mysterious blob of as yet primordial ooze. Awaiting assignment. Like universal stem cells.

Once a week Neil Sedaka goes out and liberates a capitalist. We roast him whole like the pig he is, with an apple in his mouth, and then eat him without using our hands. Again the idea is unification, wholeness (we don't disassemble the corpse) and also some hair of the dog stuff to keep us on our toes. We do this weekly, did I say that, and while we eat, we chant UNIGUY, UNIGUY. Shim's our mascot. A human version of the absolute. A being with just a body, no appendages or holes at all. I think of him like a cross between Casper the Ghost and an octopus. I don't know why. We trance out during these group be-ins. I like it a lot.

I happen to know that pretty much all matter is made out of the same stuff. These tiny little things called strange, charm and neutrinos. Objects and organisms just form and reform out of the ooze. There are certain particles that are especially attracted to other particles so that's why certain forms are really common as far as the observable universe. Like iron, the whole core of the earth is a hard iron ball and then a bunch of liquid iron around it. And hydrogen is the most common. That's what most of the stars are eating. Ninety-two percent of everything is hydrogen. It weighs ONE. A lot of people have done research around why for example humans don't just fall into a pile of iron and hydrogen. It's cuz we're in a struggle with the sun's heat apparently. The organism stays organized as long as it has a task. If I had to make a molecule out of humans . . . Ram Dass would be the proton, Barbra Streisand would be the electron, and Ted Kaczinsky as the neutron.

In moments of glee members will often yell out, "High five for Ram Dass!" and slap hands about face level. It is not that high of a five. This salutation is apparently particular to this land and this membership. They were doing it pretty often even on the very first day I arrived.

Book 4

I address the slimy aperture. "You're going to have to gnaw the limbs off of Sabbath's torso. It looks from here like he's just in a big weird tangle." No response. I scratch my balls and listen for any signs of morbidity. Pull my loincloth out of my ass crack.

I hear high-pitched whining. Fast mindless breaths. He is using up air.

"The exploited and dispossessed of this world can no longer seriously desire to get a piece of this putrefying pie, nor to take it over and 'self-manage' it!" I drone into the orifice earnestly. Behind me a tired voice, "Right on buddy."

I sprinkle a bit of soil onto the fleshy blockage. "Why'd you contact press?"

"So we can get more members. So people would know!" Strained, macho delivery.

"Listen up. If my solidarity with certain actions is critical it's because I can see calculation creeping in. If I reject all cooperation with the media it's because that power structure demands those who choose to participate in its activity to suddenly measure their words, drain them of substance, of the energy force that refuses all compromise!"

Growls from below. Humming.

Of late there's been mild divisions occurring in the community. There are the stone agers (stoners), the postindustrial scavengers (scabs), and a few of just your basic sort medieval barbarians whom we affectionately call Streisand. The scavengers have widened their foraging goals to include bits of plastic, metal, wood siding, car parts, synthetic drugs, pornography. They're generally a lot more angry than the stoners. They don't seem to have any hope. I can never tell if they're scabs cuz they have no hope, or they have no hope cuz they're scabs. They always strike me as without core, low on will and willpower.

Over at the bleachers some of the folks have broken off into effervescent trios and commenced to some serious butt sniffing. It seems invariably headed to some sort of coital feral flurry and I am melancholy about having to miss out on it.

"Stupid fucking purist troglodyte . . ." He continues to manifest an inky brattish courage that for some reason reminds me of that poopline down a shrimp.

"You're just a fucking essentialist," he adds.

"I am not!" I say and pop my finger out of my ass. "I'm the opposite!" That M the A is revealing a truer bourbonism than I have previously identified in him.

"There is no such thing as human nature . . ." He runs out of breath, sucks the heavy air back into his lungs and continues. "You idiot! There *is* no ONE truth." I finger my armpit hair casually.

"The things that are true are the *things that are true*, buddy. Just cuz you don't know what they are doesn't mean they don't exist!!"

"What good is a thing that is unknowable?" he exhorts.

"Not sure. But on the same arm, what good is a thing that is knowable?" Silence from below.

"Tell me something good, member. Did you like the feeling of the cookie cutter when it came?"

He is unrepentant. "I did, Air Supply. I DID."

"Well, I DID NOT, pal. I didn't." Long pause. We had finished simultaneously.

He is crying quietly. "I'm scared, Air Supply, please pull me out."

Silence.

Chuck Mangione, Late Zeppelin and a Streisand are stuffed under the bleachers in a throbbing gyroscopic heap. Late Zeppelin's head is banging into the aluminum bench at a pace that makes me feel like doing "The Bus Stop." I watch them for a long minute and the crickets rev up their nighttime calypso. Buttes the color of ash and pumpkin ascend until mercifully, they eclipse the sun. A totally relaxing primal event. I feel looser. The air is soft, exactly the temperature of my skin and fragrant to boot. Orange blossoms. Tuna. Whimpers, screams, yells replace the metallic fuck-gonging and before long the trio emerges into the soft dark night smiling. Stumbling on loose hips.

I soften considerably. "All right people, get the winch. Tell the other Neils to bring the truck." I take a couple of steps and notice Poco — whose penis is pushed into his body like a vagina — growl and snap the little fucker back out to a sproingy seven-incher with the aid of a handmade bladder. I stop in my tracks.

"Hold on Neil, forget the winch, let's make some cordage. Tell Yanni to kill a few squirrels. We don't have a lot of time."

Book 5

The tinder bundle is made from any kind of dry fibrous materials, like dead grass. Doobie Bros, Sonny and Cher, Ambrosia and the rest of the members start drifting into Meat Mecca for the LCD (Liberated Capitalist Dinner). I pick around behind a patch of smoke trees, find a couple of twigs. I notice Chuck Mangione looking at me out of the corner of her one good eye.

Back at the pit I get everything set up, make a bow, press the socket into the spindle and hold it with my mouth. Then back and forth. I don't rush. After a few minutes smoke starts rising from the bark. Chuck is actually smirking at this point, intently focused on my activity. Slowly, gently, I pull the board away from the bark, wave my hand over the dust and there it is, the red-orange glow of a firebead. I see Chuck Mangione through the haze of my handiwork. She winks and pokes her tongue out between the left part of her lips.

I happen to know she has part of her face that is motionless now and it will be like that for the rest of her days. The paralysis is from an old sex act injury where she collapsed of ecstasy in a standing bondage position and the collar had tightened around her neck while the person in charge of the whole thing was taking a whiz. Basically, she didn't get enough air for a few minutes one night. Her sidesmile is absolutely enchanting, though, and the long auburn curls that cascade down her back like seventy-seven waterfalls are just too much for my little body to bear. I smile back.

I cup the bundle and blow into it from underneath. One, two, three and boom, it bursts into flame right in the palm of my hand. Everyone cheers. I have created life and energy and I feel good.

We have stuffed the LC with a combination of mealworms, grasshoppers, cattail roots and mustard. His hands are starting to look a little bloated and I am relieved when we finally get him over the fire. The meal is protein heavy but most of us are a little light on our feet so it never hurts. After eating and UNIGUY chanting, I walk over and find Chuck Mangione. She's laughing with U2 who is now wearing the meat corpse's shirt. It is mostly frowned on to pilfer the civ-wear from the meat corpses but in this case we could all see the draw. Tie dye looked pretty decent on U2. In a soft way. I don't think anyone else could have pulled it off.

I kick the warm dirt. Toe a very small fragment of what appears to be colon tissue in a move that I hope comes off as humble, eager.

At a loss for propositional technical terms, I hasten a shot. "I like your fur." I poke at her hair. "Would you like to get funky with me?"

"She's a lesbian!" U2 sneers in a really nerdy voice and then cackles loudly. Chuck holds my gaze. That sidesmile is really a star up close.

"You know there's no real genders anymore," I continue.

"Yeah, I know." Her left eye is unswerving.

"Plus, my dick is so small you might mistake it for a clitoris. You wouldn't be the first."

"A micro-penis," she purrs. "That's sexy."

"I'm not kidding." I kick into Bachman Turner Overdrive and we both start to walk at the same time.

"Yeah, and you could fly a 747 into my ass opening too. . . ."

If she had two sides to her mouth they would definitely have collaborated on this particular grin. I kiss her on the motionless little flap of skin that is her right eyelid.

"Get America and Spyro Gyra into the Haystack Hut in half an hour. You'll each lose a forearm up there before you can say

'Bakunin's Revenge.'" Bakunin's Revenge is what the group calls it when a member is constipated. No one says it outright but slowness is considered a sign of faintness of heart. Lack of feral primacy, rewilding ambition. I'm proud to say I never have suffered from it.

I get over to the Roadkill Rapprochement just before she does and load up on what we call bacon fat. It's actually CEO drippings. From when we happen to liberate a CEO. And if you just want to use it as personal lubricant, it "stays good" for up to four months. In a penicillin sort of way.

Chuck Mangione shows up a few minutes late with Pablo Cruise and Joe Cocker. This really burns me up for a long minute. We whisper-argue like eviscerated rubber chickens.

"I didn't say you could bring just anyone! Pablo Cruise and Joe Cocker??" I feel totally dirty.

"Well, Air Supply, they think you're sexy." She pauses a beat for dramatic effect. "So." She sucks her good cheek into her teeth.

I abdicate. "You know the rules, though, nothing divisible by two."

So Joe Cocker watches while we get off. Concentrically abiding the mandate that we disavow his pleasure in the creation of ours. I'll just say right here that the three of us do absolutely everything that any body can do to another body. And we do it TWICE. Pablo Cruise in particular is creative. Marsupial such that takes my breath away. Shim is a nasty little pachyderm. Not trendy at all.

I'm Not Lost, I Just Don't Know Where the Fuck We Are

Rhiannon Argo

We are stranded on the side of the road on the outskirts of Paris with our suitcases and stuff scattered around us on the sidewalk. It's the third week of the Sister Spit Eurotrash tour, which is me, Michelle Tea, Cristy C. Road, Kat Marie Yoas, Amos Mac and the two Emilys. The two Emilys are from England. They have cute accents and look like cartoon characters. Emily #1 goes by Em, and she's the person who organized the tour and brought Sister Spit to Europe. Emily #2 is her friend, who was our driver when we toured around the UK, and then we missed her so much that she came to join us on the Europe leg of our tour. In Europe we had to hire a new driver, because Emily couldn't drive outside of the UK. The new driver was named Sabine and she's the one who just dumped us, and all our stuff, on the side of the road in the middle of nowhere and then drove away forever.

I am frantically looking for a place to pee. Before Sabine left us on the side of the road we were lost and driving in circles around Paris for a while with everyone in the van fighting and yelling, which was no time to request a pee stop. I'm making Amos Mac help me look for a spot, urging him to block me from traffic while I try to lodge one of those plastic things, (things that are supposed to help a female-bodied person pee standing up that I brought on this tour specifically for this sort of emergency) into the unzipped zipper of my pants. It's not working. I want to pee off the side of the road like a careless gay, but apparently you have to drop your drawers to get the thing lodged into the right spot to successfully catch your pee. I don't feel like showing all the French drivers my bare ass, so we head over to a nearby cemetery where the security guard eyes us suspiciously no matter which tombstone we try to hide behind, as if he thinks we are two French teenagers looking for a place to *fair l'amour*. I duck behind a large tomb, feeling like for sure angry French ghosts will now haunt me for the rest of my life for peeing on them. "Crazy Sabine just up and left us!" Amos says, shaking his head in disbelief.

Back at the side of the road Emily, who looks like Hailey Mills from the original *Parent Trap* movies — the cute boyish one with the blonde bowl-ish cut — holds up a map of Paris, and Em and Michelle take turns squinting at it from various angles. Kat is pacing the sidewalk in her red cowboy boots and tight black jeans, red curls springing from her head. Cristy is sitting on a short cement wall near the street looking solemn. "I even had a crush on her until she started saying those racist things," she says about Sabine.

Sabine may have been crushable for Cristy in the beginning, those first few days when she drove our van in her all black skin-tight squatter outfits and blasted Slovenian black metal as she drove through the quaint European countryside, but that was before she became a hostile scowling mess, and a terribly unreliable driver who hated us all. She had been a dark cloud hanging over our tour for the last week and although we were lost and worried about making it to our show at the legendary Parisian bookstore, *Shakespeare and Company* in a mere few hours, we were all relieved to be rid of her. *Ding-dong the witch is dead.*

We met Sabine in Slovenia, a small country in Southeastern Europe. She lived in a van in the parking lot of an artist community called Metelkova in Ljubljana. Ljubljana is a truly gorgeous gothic city with bridges guarded by fire-breathing stone dragons and castles perched in the hills above. I'd love to go back there someday, as long as I didn't run into Sabine because she might murder me by choking me to death with one of her super long ropey dreads.

The Sister Spit Euro Trash tour arrived in Ljubljana on a bright orange *Easy Jet*, which Michelle nicknamed "the Greyhound of air travel." When we arrived at the airport we were immediately amped to be in a sunshiny country. We'd just spent the first week of our tour traveling through the damply cold UK. Standing in the sunshine of the airport parking lot we wondered if Sabine was going to show up to get us. No one had actually ever met her. Em had found her on MySpace when she'd posted a bulletin looking for our European tour driver. Sabine had applied for the job claiming experience as a driver and then assisted in planning our tour route.

We were a bit wary of what she would be like. In the van back in the UK we passed around a smart phone with her MySpace picture pulled up. Sabine glared out from the screen with her hefty middle finger thrust up at the camera. Her Myspace page headline read, "Fuck Off and Die."

We were relieved when Sabine showed up at the airport. She muttered a few gruff words as she threw our bags in back of our new tour van. She was with her boyfriend and they looked like two Second Life Avatars with twin fashion, both tall, Amazon-sized, with chiseled bone structure, various piercings, very long thick black dreads and head to toe tight black clothing. They spoke non-stop in Slovenian the entire drive, only to each other, and chain-smoked cigarettes while we tried to figure out if the windows in back of the van rolled down. They didn't so we'd better get used to traveling in a second-hand smoke hotbox.

We peered through the smoky haze at Slovenia out the window as we drove, entranced by the beautiful city, and then awed by the awesome looking artist's commune we pulled up in front of. Metelkova was once military barracks and the headquarters of the Yugoslav National Army before it was squatted by artists in 1993. The artists protected the building with their own bodies when demolition balls once arrived to tear their beloved space down. Now, it looked like a magical playground, the main building covered in a huge sculpture — a massive spider web of goulash, spindly flesh-toned alien bodies — each one with a different howling, scowling, or leering face. Every surface of Metelkova was covered in sculpture, sparkling collages made from gems, vibrant paintings and massive intricate graffiti pieces. Sabine led us to our sleeping quarters, a cozy artist's studio on the top floor of the barracks. This was our first time on this tour that we'd gotten our own room to stay in, and not just a chunk of floor in someone's living room, so we were happy.

Sabine came to get us for dinner. She'd cooked for us so therefore we decided she must be nicer than our first impression. She'd made yummy pumpkin soup, vegetables, and gave us fresh bread, and coffee. Michelle speculated that surely she'd just been gruff earlier because she was trying to impress her big manly boyfriend. The only red alert during dinner was that several guys lingering around the kitchen claimed they had never seen Sabine cook and that she was merely trying to kiss our asses.

The next morning we explored Metalkova. Kat, Em, and I climbed strange structures that looked like they were part of a kid's playground designed by people on acid and Cristy found a large bearded man sitting in a jeweled throne in the parking lot that everyone called "The King" to smoke her out. Metalkova was cool but there were a handful of glaring men who wouldn't let us take any pictures. I leaned over the railing on the deck in front of our studio and watched Sabine cleaning out her house in the parking lot below. I went down to check out her home and she greeted me with a rough nod of her chin. From the outside the van looked normal, slathered in a coat of thick black paint but on the inside it was an awesome fur-lined and leopard-printed love shack, complete with a woodburning stove and animal parts such as huge black bird wings decorating the walls. Cristy came over to check out the van and I believe this is when her crush on Sabine truly began to form.

After our show in Ljubljana we drove to Vienna where we stayed in an anarchist squat housed in a huge, cold, concrete six-story building. Sabine seemed happy to be at the Squat because she got to re-unite with her people — clothed in all black clothing held together with black patches and piles of dreads on every head. While eating a yummy vegan dinner in the dining hall we tried to play a game of "find someone without dreads" and we were hard-pressed to find a dread-less head in the room. Even a few kids with short cropped or a shaved heads would eventually turn their heads to reveal one long dread growing from the back of their head in a tube shape.

The Vienna squat was dark and cold, with weird, unwelcoming energy. Kat and I found a greenhouse-roofed-type porch and sat on some plastic furniture that perhaps was some squatter's bed. The sun set over the grey buildings between the bars on the frosted windows. *Maybe this place was once a prison*, we speculated. We decided to make out to pass the time, laughing whenever a heavy booted anarchist stomped by us on the nearby stairs.

That night we performed in the squat's smoky stone basement

and later left the moshing dance party to go upstairs for lesbian ac-tivities, like drinking tea and coffee while Michelle read our tarot. Sabine was off drinking, or else perhaps Michelle would have read her Tarot and found out how dark sided she was right then and there.

The next day we drove to Munich, Germany where Amos Mac met us and joined the tour. We performed at a very loving artist space called Kafe Kult and they were very warm and nurturing, which we needed since half the tour got sick while shivering to sleep in that cold, dirty Vienna squat. Munich was great and we got several encores. On to Berlin where the tour schedule called for us only sleeping for about four hours after our show and then heading to a port town in the middle of the night to catch a ferry to Sweden. Leaving our show we noticed Sabine was drinking a beer while driv-ing us in the van. Apparently, she had called home and found out that her boyfriend had already cheated on her and she was upset. She informed us that she needed to drink the beer right that second because she was bi-polar and very angry.

Amos Mac and I didn't go to Sweden. We took a break from the tour, but I will fill you in on what happened there because that's where Sabine's true alcoholic personality was revealed and she turned on everyone.

In Sweden Sabine was supposed to sleep all day to prepare for the night drive back to the ferry home. Instead she got drunk and went to a protest, and then curled up and passed out in a bookstore window to catch an hour of sleep before the all-night drive. Tired and unprepared, she drove the van the wrong direction into the dark, scary Swedish woods for four hours where the tour was com-pletely lost and everyone was convinced they might die.

Cristy sang Green Day at the top of her lungs to keep Sabine awake. The tour finally made it to the shore but they had missed their ferry and thankfully were able to catch another one later.

Everyone was sleepless and angry and Sabine became hostile. Some things about her became clear, for instance, that perhaps she had never actually driven a tour before and she had no idea what she was doing when she prepared our tour route, and perhaps she had only driven her boyfriend's band's tour van around once to a few shows.

Amos and I met back up with the rest of our tour mates in Hamburg, Germany. We waited in the steps of the artist's commune and when our tour mates walked up from the street we could tell that something was very wrong. Everyone looked ragged, like they had survived a terrible ordeal, hair ratted, dark circles around eyes, and blank exhausted looks on their faces. We were filled in that Sabine hated them and the plan was to get away from her ASAP. Michelle and Em were on the Internet frantically pricing tickets from Germany to Paris while we waited for our show to start. We were willing to take the tour by train the rest of the way just to be rid of the angry dreaded beast, but sadly, tickets were too expensive, so we were stuck with her. The ironic thing was that Sabine was the only one on our tour making any money.

After our show Sabine informed us that she didn't want to drive us from the venue to the house where we were supposed to sleep. She wanted to go to a bar to get drunk. There was a language barrier between us and our hosts. Sabine was taking advantage of it by complaining about us in German. We could tell what she was doing, as her hands gestured wildly over at us, and she seemed to be earning their sympathy. Sabine left us and we made do, laid our sleeping bags down in an empty stone-floored room of the art commune.

In Cologne Sabine got drunk and tried to bond with us again at the Karaoke bar, even flashing us her boobs, which made us all feel awkward. She was nice to us when she was wasted, but in the morning we had a long drive to Paris and it was apparent she was hung over and angrier than ever. It took us forever to get to Paris. She was blasting Slovenian black metal and would not turn it down even when we pleaded. She would pull over on the side of the road at random rest stops, kick her feet up and chain smoke. She wasn't feeling good, she admitted. When we finally got to Paris she drove in circles around the city, and when Michelle asked her if she was lost — in an attempt to help out — Sabine screamed at us. "I'm not lost, I just don't know where the fuck we are!"

What? We were confused by that sentence.

Sabine then shouted, "You people are all talking to me at once. I'm so SICK of you people."

YOU are sick of US? We couldn't believe it! We were the ones sick of her, and with that all of our pent up feelings came forth. Cristy yelled at her for saying racist things. Everyone yelled at once. Sabine pulled that van over and screeched to a halt. We all wanted out of the van and she wanted her money. She scowled at us, standing on the side of the road making a large pile out of our bags as Michelle and Em rushed to an ATM to get her the cash she demanded. After that she wanted even more money, so there was more arguing until finally she muttered curses at us and drove away, crying.

So here we are, not lost, but perhaps not knowing where the fuck we are. We find our way to the Paris Metro where we navigate the rush hour crowds, our arms teeming with backpacks, sleeping bags and even an air mattress accidentally stolen from a Swedish host. Cristy sees a hot butch with blonde shaved hair and cute smile standing on the platform and whisper-yells to me, *She looks like a girl version of Billy Joel. I Want to Make Out With Her*! And we are in the city of love, so this seems entirely possible.

Sister Spit 2011 Tour Diary

MariNaomi

3 20 11 Day 6

We went driving in the driving rain, headed for "The Sac."

Kirk had let out a morbid fart earlier, so each nasty scent that reached our noses was suspect.

Was that you, Kirk?

No! It's cows!

Hi!

TINKERING WITH A/V EQUIPMENT

Hello!

03 * 20 * 2011   Day 6

A really nice (and adorable) gal named Sandy bought us all dinner.

SHE WAS SO NICE!

EVERYBODY THERE WAS SO NICE, IN FACT.

Maybe it was the beans, but something disagreed with me. I snuck backstage to discreetly pass gas, but...

Hi!

Do you need anything?

No! I just came back here to FART!

Oh! I'll leave you alone then!

When I shared this story with my tour mates, Kirk Read said this

So the TABLES have TURNED!

They will all know soon enough how flatulent you are, Mari-chan!

3 • 27 • 11 DAY 13 SUNDAY

after being kept up all night, the Amazing Kirk Read decided to confront the meth heads three doors down.

Blake, decked out in his new Queer Alliance T-shirt, bravely went out to back up Kirk. But Kirk was okay.

But that wasn't the end of it.

How are you?

3-28-11 8:11 PM

BACKSTAGE AT HOLOCENE IN PORTLAND, OR.

WHEN MICHELLE ACCIDENTALLY SWITCHED THE LINE-UP AND ANNOUNCED TO THE AUDIENCE THAT KIRK WAS ON FIRST, HE FRANTICALLY CHANGED INTO HIS COSTUME—A MULLET WIG, BIG GLASSES, AND SKIN-TIGHT ZEBRA PRINT JUMPSUIT.

4 · 3 · 11 Day 20

The plane ride was SCARY.

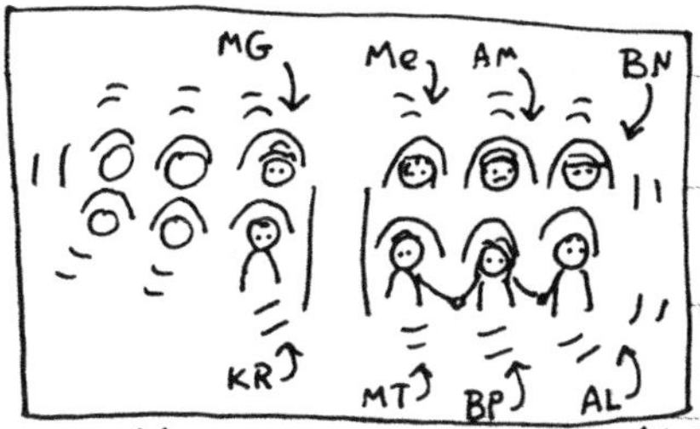

mid-flight, it felt like we were being whipped around in the sky. So much turbulence!

My iPod was on "shuffle" but I quickly searched through my songs for an empowering playlist.

we survived though. Obviously.

at our hotel, I suffered the time difference.

4·4·11   Day 21

There was some tension in the van when jet lag and miscommunication led to us leaving 20 minutes later than scheduled.

Passing Thru Manhattan got me nostalgic, and upstate NY was foresty and magical.

Manhattan Skyline

Yony's back!

Amos, this drive is making me jealous that you're moving here.

Upon arriving to our hotel, there was some drama when poor, sick Myriam made a text-etiquette blunder.

I accidentally sent a shit-talking text to the person I was talking shit about!

Strangely, when she called her partner TJ, it turns out TJ had done the same thing!

"utter twattiness"

Tweet

4 9 11   10:09PM

Hi!

KIRK EATING THE FEATHER IN MY HAIR
AT A DINER. THIS WAS EVEN BEFORE HIS FOOD
WAS ABOMINABLY LATE.

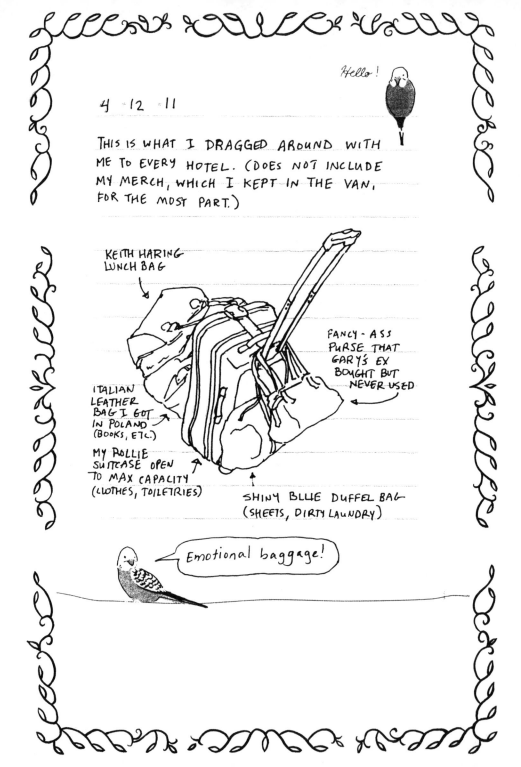

Hello!

4·12·11

THIS IS WHAT I DRAGGED AROUND WITH ME TO EVERY HOTEL. (DOES NOT INCLUDE MY MERCH, WHICH I KEPT IN THE VAN, FOR THE MOST PART.)

KEITH HARING LUNCH BAG

FANCY-ASS PURSE THAT GARY'S EX BOUGHT BUT NEVER USED

ITALIAN LEATHER BAG I GOT IN POLAND (BOOKS, ETC.)

MY ROLLIE SUITCASE OPEN TO MAX CAPACITY (CLOTHES, TOILETRIES)

SHINY BLUE DUFFEL BAG (SHEETS, DIRTY LAUNDRY)

Emotional baggage!

4·14·11 Day 31

another early morning with a long drive ahead, but we couldn't wait to exit that hotel.

"Hello!"

There was ejaculate on my headboard. I spent the night curled up in a fetal position in the middle of the bed.

MICHELLE WITH A VICTORY-INN PTSD

I had gas pains during the entire drive, but I didn't allow myself to fart in the midst of all those people.

Blake read aloud from Andrew Shaffer's book, Philosophers who Failed at Love. Michelle read aloud a Jonathan Franzen piece in the New Yorker, which put most of us to sleep.

I was further relaxed by a warm bath in a tub that probably never contained a dismembered human body (unlike the last creepy hotel we stayed in).

DON'T COUNT ON IT!

About the Authors

Samuel Topiary is an interdisciplinary media artist, performer, filmmaker and writer based in Brooklyn, NY. She studied playwriting at the NYU Dramatic Writing Program, received an MFA in Film/Video from Bard College and has created music videos for Le Tigre.

Cooper Lee Bombardier is a writer and visual artist living in Portland. His writing has appeared in *Pathos Literary Journal* and the anthologies *The Lowdown Highway, From the Inside Out*, and *Trans/Love*.

Blake Nelson is an author of adult and children's literature. His first novel *Girl* was excerpted in the magazine *Sassy* in three successive issues and later adapted into a film. He is based in Los Angeles.

Eileen Myles is an award-winning poet and author based in New York. She has published more than a dozen volumes of poetry and fiction including *Not Me, Chelsea Girls, Cool for You*, and *Skies*.

Ali Liebegott is the recipient of the Lambda Literary Award for her book *The Beautifully Worthless*. She currently lives in San Francisco.

Tamara Llosa-Sandor is a former news reporter now exploring the murky terrain between memoir and fiction. She holds an MFA in creative writing from Columbia University. Her first book, *As Filipino As Fruitcake*, may or may not be published by 2018.

Nicole J. Georges is a Portland-based zinester whose recent comic *Invincible Summer* was collected into an anthology and released as two volumes from Tugboat Press and Microcosm Publishing.

Tara Jepsen is a writer and performer from San Francisco, now living in Los Angeles. Her short stories have been published in the anthologies *Pills, Thrills, Chills and Heartache* and *It's So You: 35 Women on Fashion and Style*.

Ben McCoy is a writer and performance artist living in San Francisco and is featured in the anthology *Persistence: All Ways Butch and Femme*.

Beth Lisick is a performer and New York Times bestselling author of the comic memoir *Everybody Into the Pool* and the gonzo self-help manifesto *Helping Me Help Myself*. She currently resides in New York.

Michelle Tea is the author of four memoirs, a collection of poetry and two novels, most recently the young adult fantasy tale *A Mermaid in Chelsea Creek*. She co-founded Sister Spit in 1993, and revived it in 2007. Michelle is Executive Director of the literary non-profit RADAR Productions, and the editor of Sister Spit Books, an imprint of City Lights.

Cristy C Road is based in New York and is the author of the comics *Indestructible* and *Bad Habits*.

Harry Dodge is a Los Angeles-based visual artist, filmmaker, writer, and performer whose work has shown in national galleries including Yerba Buena Center for the Arts, P.S. 122, and The Getty.

Rhiannon Argo is the recipient of the Lambda Literary Award for her novel *The Creamsickle*. Her work has also been published in *Baby Remember My Name: New Queer Girl Writing*, and *It's So You: 35 Women on Fashion, Beauty and Personal Style*. She currently lives in San Francisco.

MariNaomi lives in San Francisco and is the author and illustrator of the graphic memoir *Kiss & Tell: A Romantic Resume, Ages 0 to 22*.

Kat Marie Yoas is a San Francisco-based author. Her essays can be found in *Not Another Wave: Dispatches from the Next Generation of Feminists* and *It's So You: 35 Women on Fashion and Style.*

Sara Seinberg is a San Francisco writer, performer, and visual artist. Her photography has appeared in *Ms. Magazine*, the *Village Voice*, and *TimeOUT New York.*

Kirk Read is the author of *How I Learned to Snap*, which has been named an American Library Association Honor Book. He lives in San Francisco.

Elisha Lim is a Toronto-based artist and author of the graphic novel *100 Butches.*

Lenelle Moise is a poet, playwright, and performance artist living in Northampton, MA. Her poems and essays have been featured in several anthologies including *Word Warriors: 35 Women Leaders in the Spoken Word Revolution.*

Myriam Gurba is the author of *Dahlia Season* and *Wish You Were Me*, and has been included in the anthology *Life As We Show It* and *Ambientes*. She lives in Los Angeles.

Cassie J. Sneider grew up in the murky depths of Lake Ronkonkoma, New York, a town with a haunted lake, a trailer park, and a record store. She put 240,000 miles on a Toyota Echo doing readings all over the country. She has been published in *the2ndhand, Sadie Magazine, Newsday, Savage Love*, and when she was eleven, Ann Landers' advice column. She has a B.A. in English that she has often thought about while working at bookstores and strip clubs, and once, when she found it in a broken frame under a box of old lottery tickets and Christmas ornaments at her mom's house. Cassie J. Sneider collects 8-tracks and new friends. She is author and illustrator of *Fine, Fine Music.*